MADS ON MIC

L. CLARA

Mads On Mic

L. Clara

Contents

A note from L. Clara

Before you start, I want to take a moment to say thank you to the authors and narrator who allowed me to include fictional versions of them in this story. K. D. Smalls, Katie A. Perez, Aoife Rye, Nikki Grant, and Lauren Beck. Y'all are amazing friends, and I adore each of you so much!

Additionally - Bronze Fox Boutique, who gave me the ok to include one of my favorite t-shirts for Mads' wardrobe, which is from their incredible shop!

Content Warnings

Loss of employment

Cyber/Social Media Stalking - but make it awkward

Mention of SA

Mention of Real-life Stalking

Bullying

Sexually Explicit Content

Assault

For the women who have found themselves between the pages

Have you ever had an out-of-body experience? You know, a moment where you feel like you've got to be someone else watching the train wreck unraveling before you, instead of experiencing it because there's no way it could be real life? Yeah, that's how I'm feeling right now.

"Hi, Maddox. We appreciate the past five years that you've been loyal to this company. You've been an incredible asset to us over that time; however, we have made the difficult decision to end our professional relationship."

My eyes are locked on the screen where my boss, Mack, who I also thought was a friend for as long as we've been working together, and the human resources manager are pictures in the tiny square of the video chat. Both of them have blank stares on their faces as if they're using emotion-suppressing software instead of blurring their backgrounds to-day. I grip my chest trying to steady the chaos happening inside.

"Why? I've been your top graphic designer for the last four years." I say, with a confidence in my voice I don't feel. "I've had no disciplinary actions taken against me; I've been ahead of every deadline that you've given me."

My boss – well ex-boss now, I guess – opens her mouth to speak but is immediately cut off by the HR manager. I think her name is Pam, at least according to the little tag under her video feed.

"It's nothing personal; we've had to eliminate a number of positions, yours being one of them." Her snarky response comes out in a nasally tenor, which makes my blood boil.

My eyes squint into slivers while shooting daggers back at her. I sit back and cross my arms under my chest not taking my eyes off the screen; I remain silent until they provide further instruction.

"Uh – anyway, you will receive one year of severance pay since you've been with us for so long." Pam's matter-of-fact tone keeps me quiet. "I expect you to box up and ship back your computer and any other equipment we've provided during your employment."

"Sure, as soon as you send me the box and a shipping label." I snap at her, in shock that she would insinuate that I'd be neglectful in returning equipment when I've been nothing but a stellar employee since they hired me.

"Of course," Pam rolls her eyes when Mack answers for her.

Without uttering another word, the video feeds go black and they are gone. I click through the sequence to shut off all my equipment and stare at the dark screen, my heart in my throat. I've been with this company since I graduated from college; never in my wildest dreams would I have expected this to happen with how often they praise my work.

"Aaaggghhh," I bury my face in my hands letting out the frustrated scream that I had been holding back during the latter part of the call.

Anger radiates through me while I sit on my couch sulking over what's happened. My thoughts spiral down a rabbit hole, thinking about the what if's that I'm going to need to deal with over the days to come. It's making my nerves a wreck. Sure, my severance will allow me the time to find my dream job, but this is so out of left field that it's difficult to comprehend what those next steps might even be.

When I finally emerge from my apartment an hour later, the sun is beginning to set in the distance and a beautiful combination of orange, pink, and purple decorates the horizon. I let out a long sigh and try to find the positive in the situation.

My feet carry me down the street, unsure of where I'm headed. I just needed to roam after feeling so much emotion in such a short amount of time. A cool breeze brushes over me, leaving a trail of goosebumps along my arms. I glance up, rubbing my hands against my chilled skin, to see a sign in the window of the small dance studio for a new fitness dance class.

Her Final Shot - The Musical: a class inspired by the new hit Broadway show.

If I'm honest, I've never seen the show. The only reason I know it exists at all is because my best friend Ka'Mani is huge into theatre and lives in New York City. This may be the closest I'll get to seeing it for a while.

Having worked from home for so long, I've lived a sedentary life. I've always been a big girl, but I've definitely seen healthier days. My lips twist into a smile when I glance down at my outfit, internally patting myself on the back for living in yoga pants because I'm ready for the class. I pull open the glass door of the studio and step inside.

"Hey Mads, how can I help you?" My smile grows wider at the greeting from Jayne, the owner of the studio, and an old friend from high school. This town is so small you can't do anything without everyone knowing about it.

"I'd like to do the class that starts tonight." I stand tall, my shoulders pushed back and my head held high.

"You're lucky; we have one spot left." Jayne's lips turn up at the corners as she types away on her computer. "Head on in and we'll be getting started in a few minutes."

She gestures to the door behind her, which leads into the studio. I walk through to find my landlord, Elle, and her best friend, Fallon, among a handful of other familiar faces. They wave me over to join them, but before we can say much more than hello, a speaker cracks to life with the instructor's voice as they step onto the stage at the front of the room.

At the start of the class, I have no clue what I'm in for. Sure, I know the album is almost as popular as the show and the music is upbeat, a mix between hip hop and pop music, but I don't recall anyone ever talking about the story.

Tears stream down my cheeks when the voice of lead character Monica declares she will find the person responsible for killing her father, the chief of police, and make them face the consequences. Let's be real here, it's not really about the father or the fact that he's a police officer that has me feeling so much emotion – it's the lyrics she's belting out in the most sensational voice I've heard. Really, she could put Idina Menzel to shame.

Today is my day; you will not keep me away.

I will not be shamed today or any day.

I will make you proud; make me proud before the end of days.

Something about those words makes my heart beat so erratically in my chest. They inspire me to take a chance on myself. For the past year, I've been toying with the idea of creating a podcast to celebrate my love of smutty romance books and how it has created a sex-positive outlook for women.

What? I may be single, but I know what I want, and when I find a partner again, I will not hesitate to speak up. That's all because of this genre of romance, and I know others have had that epiphany too.

I continue following the movements that the instructor is demonstrating at the front of the class. By the time the class ends, my tears have dried and I've got a smile on my face that could rival that of a teacher on the last day of school. It's time to start *"O"-The Positive Side of Smut.*

Chapter One

One year later

"Buzz buzz, Bitches. Buzz, buzz, Bitches." My favorite line from an audiobook, *The Unexpected Match* – I immediately made it my ringtone when the audio was released – repeats on a loop while I stare at my screen typing up a proposal for a new sponsor. A soft smile dances across my lips when I see, Ka'Mani, is calling. I swipe to answer, thankful I have my earbud in when her beautiful face fills the screen.

Seriously, video calls are the best invention in the modern world.

"Hey girl! Happy almost birthday!" Unable to take my eyes from the phone, as I take in her beauty; the tone of her flawless skin reminds me of a deep umber. She easily puts mainstream beauty standards to shame.

Even though she still has her bright pink satin bonnet on since she hasn't done her makeup yet this morning. I've never seen someone so beautiful. Really, it's annoying because she doesn't realize how stunning she is.

"Don't 'hey girl' me; you are number one on the freaking podcast chart for your category!" Ka'Mani squeals so loudly I have to pull the tiny speaker out of my car. There is an unmistakable pride in her bright smile when she talks about my ranking. Her gaze remains on me while she meticulously applies her foundation, watching the embarrassment color my face. I've not been able to easily accept praise in my work after being fired. Before that fateful day just over a year ago, I would boast about my accomplishments. But now even acknowledging a little bit of success makes me nervous.

My cheeks heat. I know the podcast has been doing incredibly well, especially with how young it is. While I may bust my ass every day to make sure I stay relevant and continue to work with high-end sponsors, it's not lost on me that I got lucky in the beginning. I had a huge opportunity to interview a few big names early on, and it definitely helped me take off.

"Holy shit. I didn't realize they'd updated the charts." Tears prick at the corners of my eyes while I think back over the past year. "I had a feeling I was going to get above top five, but number freaking one!"

The two of us take turns squealing into the phone and then take a few moments to calm down enough to hold a conversation.

"Girl, I miss you." Ka'Mani taps her long emerald fingernails against her lip before she breaks out in a ridiculous grin. "Why don't you come out to the city for my birthday next week! I haven't seen you in forever!"

My mouth pops open, and I'm ready to decline like I have every year before because I couldn't get time off. When I realize my new reality, a wide smile spreads across my face.

"I'll buy tickets as soon as we get off the phone!" There's an excitement in my voice I haven't heard in a while as I confirm I'll be there.

The rumbling vibration from the train as we edge closer to Penn Station has kept my anxiety at bay. I've never been a fan of flying; sure, trains may take longer, but it's a much more relaxing experience. There's Wi-Fi too, so I can work while I travel. It's a win-win.

I've spent most of the twenty-hour trip editing the last-minute podcast I recorded with one of my author friends, who has an upcoming release next week. It's perfect timing for both of us because she'll get extra promo and I'll get to spend the week in the city not prepping for a new show. My heart lurches in my chest when a squeal and crackle sound over the intercom before a voice from a crew member begins to speak.

"We will be arriving at our final destination, Penn Station, in twenty minutes. Please have all of your belongings ready to disembark. All doors will be opening." The announcement is repeated several times before a final click echoes over the sound system, and we're met with silence overhead.

I let out a shaky breath. Something about that squeal scared the shit out of me. Zero out of ten, don't recommend. Once I've got everything saved and social media posts scheduled to tease the upcoming episode, I shut down my laptop and close it before sliding it back into my backpack. I stand to grab my bag from the overhead bin when a gorgeous guy steps up next to me and pulls it down. A smirk plays on my lips when I glance up into his beautiful green eyes.

"Thanks."

"Anytime, gorgeous." His gaze rakes down my body appreciatively. "Are you visiting or coming home?" His smooth voice does things to my nerves that make me glad I brought my vibrator.

"Dumbass, you're engaged to my baby sister. Stop flirting." Another tall, muscular man walks up behind him and smacks the stranger upside his head. His eyes bore into the side of my face, which is heating under his gaze. No clue why *I'm* embarrassed when I did nothing wrong. Ahh, the life of a woman.

Instead of continuing the conversation, I shove my arms through the straps of my backpack. Once I've got it situated comfortably on my shoulders, I pull the handle out from the top of my suitcase and wheel it toward the door.

Stepping off the train and onto the bustling platform, I'm immediately encased by so many people, which has both my excitement and anxiety mounting. "This is going to take some getting used to," I chuckle to myself. I wrap my fingers tightly around the handle and follow the signs to the exit. After a quick ride up an escalator, I find myself surrounded by shops and small restaurants, all still inside the station. This place is huge compared to the small transit platform I left from in Hollow Heights. I'm taken aback by how unprepared I am for it.

When I finally reach the exit, I take a deep breath and take my first step outside since yesterday. I stop and stare up at the immense buildings surrounding me. There's more stories than there is sky and more people on the sidewalks than there are cars on the street.

"Holy shit." I gasp. "I'm not in Kansas anymore."

It takes a beat before I regain control of myself. When I realize I've been standing in place looking around like an obvious idiot and tourist, I step off to the side to pull my phone free from my pocket. I send a quick message to Ka'Mani to let her know I arrived safely. She was shocked when I told how long I'm staying since I'm on my own. If she didn't have to save her PTO for her wedding next year, I know she'd have me stay with her and take the week off to hang out with me. As much as I'd enjoy the extra time with her, it's my first time on vacation since I've been an adult. I'm looking forward to spending some time exploring on my own.

After finding the address of the small studio apartment I rented for the week, I enter the information into my GPS app. I'm happy to see it truly is only a ten-minute walk from the station and set off towards my destination. The sights that encompass me with every step I take make me that much more eager to explore the city this week. A lightness fills my chest when I reach the apartment I'll call home for the duration of my visit.

The building access code allows me to pass through the narrow entryway from the crowded street into a quieter space on the other side. I let out a breath of relief; thankful to see that there are clear signs directing me toward my unit on the third floor. A soft giggle passes my lips, thankful I've kept doing the dance classes. A year ago, I never would have wanted to climb three flights of stairs. Today though, my eyes drift up the steps, and a proud smile spreads when I begin to ascend without a worry of losing my breath. I'm by no means thin. The polite way to describe my body type is curvy. I'm a big girl, and I'm ok with that. It only takes a few minutes to reach my door, and the second entry code works for that just as easily as the one downstairs.

It's a tiny ten by ten room with a full-size bed, small desk, bathroom, and even smaller kitchenette; it's perfect for what I need. Once I tuck my bag out of the way, I sit on the bed and check the time. It's only eleven in the morning.

"Hmm," I ponder while I tap on the phone screen, pulling up the times of upcoming performances of *Her Final Shot.*

Obviously, it's on my to-do list this week.

I'm amazed to see that there is one seat left in the first row for the matinee this afternoon, and at a ridiculously low price.

Hell, yes.

I click purchase and head back outside to meander around a bit before the show. I'm pleasantly surprised to find the theatre is only a few blocks away. It's not shocking that I'm the first one in line waiting to enter; given how close I'm staying to the venue. A crowd begins to form behind me as the time gets closer to the show starting, and I turn to find a woman wearing a dirty thirty birthday sash.

"Happy birthday!" I chuckle when I take in the bright smile on her face. We exchange pleasantries for a while until the doors open. She shares that it's her fifth time seeing the show. I envy her ability to come so often until she shares that she's from across the river in Jersey. There is an awkward silence after that realization, neither of us making eye contact again.

Why do I feel like the ghost of Alexander Hamilton laughing at me right now?

Like whoever is working the front of the line has a direct connection to my soul, the doors open when I turn back around. My cheeks hurt from how hard I'm smiling as I make my way through the security. I pause to take in the beauty of the theatre's lobby once I get my ticket scanned. The space looks every bit as regal as you'd expect, and yet, nothing could prepare me for just how truly spectacular this place is. When I cross the open hall, my eyes land on the merch counter, which is already surrounded by ticket holders. I'd say merch has never been my thing, but I'd be lying. I just don't feel like waiting in line any longer.

My seat is incredibly easy to find once I enter the room where the magic happens.

I glance at my watch to see I still have thirty minutes before the show starts, so I take the time to reply to messages and comments from my subscribers and potential sponsors for upcoming podcast episodes. Affiliate marketing is where it's at for me–as far as being able to make a living out of my chosen profession, so I do my best not to keep any companies waiting long when they reach out.

When the lights dim, I silence my phone and shove it into my bag, ready to see the show that changed my life a year ago.

The entire experience goes by in a flash. The performance is better than I could have hoped for. Sure, I knew the storyline from the number of times I've listened to the album but seeing it play out on the stage in front of me has my heart so full.

Tears fill my eyes when the song that altered my entire world in the best of ways begins. I quietly sob into my sweater sleeve when the actress playing Monica sings the lines that continue to resonate with me every day. I wipe my face dry and lock eyes with the male lead for half a second before the room is shrouded in darkness. When the lights come back on the entire cast is there, taking their final bow. It's a strange feeling, having so many positive emotions, but being unable to stop the tears from flowing.

I pull my phone out and snap a selfie of myself in front of the stage for my own memories. As I slide the device back into my bag, I feel a gentle tap on my shoulder and turn around to see one of the company actors still in costume with a shy smile on her face.

"Hey, can you come with me?"

Chapter Two

I nearly stumble over myself when I see a raven-haired knockout center stage, in the first row. Her beauty is an all-consuming kind that will make you forget your own name. How I get through my lines without an error is beyond me.

There is a moment when I'm able to run backstage briefly before the curtain call instead of waiting in the wings, and tonight, I take the opportunity.

"I am not exaggerating when I say the most beautiful woman I have ever seen is sitting in the first row." I say in a rush to Cassie, one of the company cast members, as soon as I step backstage after my final solo of the night.

She and Annie have become two of my best friends since we all started the show around the same time. Cassie snorts and rolls her eyes. She's usually the one who drools over audience members while I try to steer clear. Every time I step foot outside of the theatre, fans swarm me.

Don't get me wrong, I love the fans; they are the reason the show is still going. And let's be real – they are the reason I got the gig. But there are fans and then there are the rabid women and men who are trying to warm my bed for the night, and I've never been one for casual fucks.

I'm a serial monogamous man through and through.

"I need to meet her." I place my hands on Cassie's shoulders and stare pleadingly into my friend's eyes. "Can you please get her backstage after the curtain call?"

Cassie takes a step back, her green eyes going wide as she stares up at me.

"You're serious?" She gasps.

My lips pull into a smile.

"Like a heart attack." I squeeze her shoulders with excitement as I describe the woman I need to know. "She's wearing a red sweater that's hanging off her shoulder. Long black hair, the sweetest smile."

"Ok, who are you and what did you do to my friend?" Cassie pushes me away and silently shoos me back toward the stage for the curtain call.

The stage lights are out, leaving an illusion of darkness for the audience until the entire cast is on stage, standing side by side. I'm thankful when I feel Cassie next to me. Suddenly, we're all visible to the audience, and a roar of applause echoes through the theatre.

I glance down at Cassie, who barely reaches my chest, squeezing her hand, and flick my eyes down to the woman I was talking about. She nods a confirmation, so subtly no one will notice if they're not looking for it. She and the rest of the company rush off the stage, allowing the main cast to take our final bow. Another round of thunderous applause sounds before we're heading off the stage to change.

We've got it down to a science of stripping out of our costumes and dressing in street clothes. I already told Marie, my leading lady, that I would join her at the stage door after the matinee performance. Usually, I do enjoy the few moments of connecting with the fans after, but today, I can't shake *her* from my mind.

Finally, after the longest ten minutes of my life - ok, I'm being dramatic, it was closer to five minutes - I'm back inside. My feet move with a mind of their own toward where I know Cassie will have taken her. When I round the corner, I expect to find Cassie and my mystery woman. But I see not only Cassie, but Annie, and a handful of the cast and crew members.

My eyes land on the woman I have been infatuated with since I first stepped on stage tonight. She's even more breathtaking this close. She's easily five-seven. And outside of the stage lights, I can tell the red sweater is actually burgundy. It hangs off her right shoulder; the creamy, smooth expanse of her skin on full display. Damn. I want to bury my face there and see how sensitive her sweet flesh is.

"Holy shit, I thought you looked familiar!" I hear my friend, Annie's voice, so high-pitched with excitement it startles me.

I pause when I realize she's surrounded by my friends. They're not just introducing themselves; they're fawning over her. Which – ok I get it.

"I have been watching you since the second episode." Annie gushes, "Your interview with Katie A. Perez about her Acadia series was incredible. Do you know when her next book is coming out?"

The fuck?

Who is this beauty?

"Hey," I step forward, interrupting the conversation, knowing damn well if I allow Annie to get started talking about books I'll never get a chance to introduce myself. "I'm Dylan."

The raven-haired stunner glances up at me with a shy smile. Her eyes are dark brown, almost black. Although they don't give me Supernatural demon vibes, there's a softness to them that sends a warmth through me. I close the distance between us and extend my arm, offering my hand to her in greeting.

"Hi, I'm Maddox," a sweet pink tinge brightens her cheeks when she continues, "but everyone calls me Mads." She accepts my hand graciously, not batting an eye when I step into her space, cupping her hand between mine.

My gaze stays focused on her; our surroundings fade into the background while I take in her every feature. Mads' smile grows wider, yet I can still sense the shyness.

I open my mouth, ready to ask her to stay with me until the next show, when I feel her tense.

A familiar throat clears, causing my own shoulders to tighten. My head falls forward with frustration. I can imagine the bitchy glare she's giving Maddox. She can be so manipulative it pisses me off.

"Who are you?" Marie taunts Maddox as she steps closer, invading our space.

I roll my eyes and turn around to face my co-star with a fire in my gaze.

"Marie, this is my friend. Mads." The glare I aim at her does nothing to stop her toxic behavior.

"Yeah, you don't belong here. Go away." Her arms cross over her chest with a *don't test me* look in her eyes.

Fuck me. Why is she like this?

I spin on my heel to see Maddox with defeat etched across her beautiful features.

"Of course, it was a pleasure meeting all of you." She has a confidence about her that makes my dick swell in my pants. "The show is incredible."

Before I can open my mouth to ask her to stay and ignore Marie, Mads rushes into the maze of backstage hallways to find the exit. I groan and face Marie again.

"Why are you such a bitch?" The question comes out as a feral growl.

I'm done with her bullshit. If a woman ever visits, that isn't blood related to someone on the cast or crew, she becomes absolutely vicious.

Giving Marie no time to respond, I take off in the same direction as Mads. Knowing this place like the back of my hand, it's easy to find her just as she steps outside. Unfortunately for me, there is still a crowd of people hovering by the stage door.

God damnit.

"Hi, thank you all so much for being here. I actually need to catch up with someone." I smile and carefully push my way through the crowd as politely as I can without outwardly telling them to piss off. Unfortunately, it's such a busy time of day the sidewalks are jam-packed with pedestrians. I see a glimpse of her burgundy sweater and then nothing.

Maddox is gone.

Chapter Three

There is still a fire under my skin heating my face when I reach the stage door. A thunderous cheer startles the shit out of me when I finally step outside, only to be followed by a chorus of disappointed "boos" when the crowd realizes I'm no one special. Like Moses and the Red Sea, they part immediately to allow me through without a second thought only to surround the door again.

I pick up the pace to get away from the building, in need of a breath. When I cross 46th Street and feel enough space between myself and the theatre, I allow myself to slow. Running isn't me; it hasn't been me for a while, but the entire experience backstage was overwhelming.

The show was better than I could have ever hoped. It wasn't until after that things went sideways. My heart swells in my chest at the memory of Cassie pulling me backstage. Everyone I met, at first, was magnificent, add on the fact that more than a few of them knew me from my podcast.

I shake my head in disbelief at the memory; on top of that – the male lead approached me. Yes, I'm attractive. I've done well for myself when I've been open to dating. But for someone with any bit of celebrity to their name wanting to interact with me is just jarring. Not in a bad way, it's just shocking.

Dylan is sexy as hell; there's no other way to describe him. Sure, seeing him on stage, he's gorgeous, but the moment I saw him out of costume. My God. No one could compare in their wildest dreams. He towers over me, standing at least six foot four. He's ripped, sure he was dressed in a T-shirt, but that thing was hanging on for dear life the way it clung so snugly against his skin.

Unfortunately, the woman whose voice has been on repeat in my ears for the past year, Marie Bates, is the one who ruined it. One look at me, and her hackles rose and claws came out ready to shred me to pieces in front of the lot of them. I still don't know what caused her animosity. Was it just me or is she like that with everyone?

I blow out a shaky breath, more than a little disappointed that the person that voiced my life-changing moment turned out to be a bust.

Glancing at my watch, I see it's only four in the afternoon. I pull my phone from my bag once again to see what's close by. I may not have planned on doing anything today other than just getting to my rental and relaxing until tomorrow, but after whatever the hell happened back at Hayden-Gilmore Theatre I don't want to be alone.

When I see there is an evening cruise around Manhattan Island in half an hour, my lips turn up into a grin. Sounds like a great way to spend my evening until dinner. I set the address in my GPS before purchasing my ticket and then I'm on my way.

My feet move quickly, carrying me along to my destination. I'm not used to the beauty of the architecture I pass with every step. I'm so used to my small town and being surrounded by more farmland and pumpkin patches than cityscapes. Even in college, it was a small college town, nothing remotely close to this. There are restaurants upon restaurants and shops on top of shops. Sometimes literally – they're stacked on top of each other. I can't help but feel like a fish out of water, although I'm enjoying the change of pace more than I thought I would.

I'm pleased when I make the estimated twenty-minute walk in only fifteen.

The Circle Line ticket and information center is bustling with people when I approach.

"Ticket holders straight through, please." An older woman dressed in khakis and a hunter green polo shouts from the entryway.

I make my way down the pier where the boat I'm scheduled to board waits; cool air bounces off the water and sends a chill through my body. Glancing around, I see that most of the seats inside are full. I follow the signs to the second level and take a seat near the railing.

Violent vibration rumbles beneath my feet as the boat begins to drift out into the harbor. I can feel the excitement written across my face. I've never seen anything so immense as this city and seeing it from this angle is even more breathtaking than walking around the streets. The sun begins to set about halfway through the trip, a vision of blues, pinks and oranges blending in the horizon.

"If you direct your attention to the right, we have a fairly well-known landmark coming up – you may have heard of her." The tour guide jokes.

The Statue of Liberty comes into view as the guide speaks, and I can't help the gasp that escapes from my lips. I feel a stutter in my chest as I take in the vision before me. She's beautiful; a warm light illuminates her from underneath. I'm unable to take my eyes off the piece of history as we inch closer.

Wow.

My phone vibrates in my pocket, dragging me out of the experience. I curse under my breath when I remember I should be documenting for social media. That is my job after all.

Shit.

I record a video and take a few pictures for my social media before we pass by. When it's out of sight I look for the notification that pulled my attention from the statue and see a new message request on InstaPic.

@AnnieOnStage:

> Hey Mads! I can't believe you were here today! Thank you for coming back to meet us. I am so sorry about Marie. She can be…well, the behavior you had the displeasure of experiencing was very normal for her. Either way, I am so sorry on her behalf. I can't wait to hear your next episode. Hope to see you again before you leave!

My eyes well up with tears when I read her message; a soft chuckle escapes me when I remember this afternoon. Sure, I've had success with my Podcast and as an influencer, if that's what you want to call me, but that was the first time a group of strangers had ever come up to me in public to talk about the show or books. I send a quick response as we're pulling back into the port.

@OPosSideOfSmut:

> Thanks Annie, I loved meeting you too. I'd love to get together and chat before I go. Let me know what your schedule is like!

My ass is beginning to fall asleep with how long I've been sitting on this bar stool. I wiggle around a little to get the blood flowing while I finish typing up my day one dump post for my InstaPic.

"Hey gorgeous." I glance up away from my phone to see Levi, the handsome bartender, who has been waiting on me like I'm the only customer sitting at his bar when the entire place is packed. "Would you like another drink?"

I chuckle at the brazen way he's flirting with me. Before my response can pass my lips, my phone vibrates in my hand with a new message notification.

Fuck.

@DylanBryantOfficial:

Mads - I hate that I didn't get to message you earlier. I am horrified at Marie's behavior this afternoon. I'd love to meet you for a blue velvet to make up for it since we didn't get a chance to chat.

How the hell.

@OPosSideOfSmut:

How did you find my page?

Who says I'm drinking a blue velvet?

I toss my phone down on the counter and wave Levi back over to me.

"Hey babe. I'll take my check, please." I remain calm as I make my request. I glance over my shoulder to see if Dylan is here, which thankfully he's not, at least not that I can see.

Levi settles my bill and when he slides the receipt to me, I notice his number is on a piece of paper along with my change. I wink at him before shoving it all in my purse. When I step outside, I begin to walk the short block back to my place. I refuse to read his response to my messages until I am safely inside my building.

I close out of all the other apps except where he messaged me.

@DylanBryantOfficial:

> Annie gave it to me as soon as we stepped off stage. I didn't even change to my street clothes before I messaged you.

> Uh you just posted that's what you were drinking?

A shaky breath flows from my lungs when I see his response, and I let out a relieved laugh. I tap on my screen to pull up InstaPic and see, sure enough, I posted my photo dump without realizing it. He's not stalking me, ok, good.

Don't get me wrong, I love a good dark romance - but not in real life. Thank you.

@OPosSideOfSmut:

> I'm already back at my place for the week. I appreciate the offer though *smiley face*

@DylanBryantOfficial:

> Fair enough, I should get some rest too. How about breakfast?

Chapter Four

Three bouncing dots have been floating across my screen for the past five minutes with no response coming through. I blow out an anxious breath.

Say something.

I groan, dragging my hand through my hair.

You'd think after the number of women that have come on to me, there would be no anxiety behind talking to one. And you would be wrong – the possibility of her rejecting me is nerve-wracking.

You're sweet! I actually have a sunrise tour with Central Carriage tomorrow morning through Central Park.

A wicked grin spreads across my face at her response.

I've heard great things about that tour. I hope you have a good time. Maybe we can have breakfast after?

I don't wait for a reply before I exit out of the message and pull up an internet browser. Ready to deep-dive into the company that she is going on the tour with. She may not have meant to share that bit of information, but I'm going with it.

The internet is an interesting place. You can find anything with just a little bit of patience and a credit card to pay to unlock someone's contact information.

I tap the home phone number for Mr. Jefferson Phillips – the owner of Central Carriage – as soon as it's revealed and – not so – patiently wait while the line connects. A shrill ring repeats for longer than you'd expect someone to be able to sleep through their phone ringing.

"Someone better be dead," a gruff voice answers.

Finally.

"Hi, Mr. Phillips. I'm sorry for bothering you so late. My name is Dylan Bryant." I begin. Before I can get to why I'm calling, I hear a woman squeal in the background.

"Christ, woman, will you put your panties back on?" His reaction is a muffled growl. My lips twist into a smirk when he redirects his words back to me. "Can I help you with something, Mr. Bryant?"

"I am hoping you can. See, you have a guest tomorrow morning for the sunrise tour." I feel a heat in my cheeks. This is the first time I've gone to such great lengths to see someone again. "We were interrupted by an –" I debate how to explain the situation – "obnoxious bystander when we met. And she's only in town for a limited time."

There is a beat of silence, and I pull the phone from my ear to make sure the line hasn't disconnected; it's so quiet. Swallowing hard, nervous about his pending response, I open my mouth to plead my case when he finally speaks.

"If my wife weren't as big of a fan of yours as she is, I'd tell you to piss off." Someone, who I assume is his wife, audibly swoons somewhere close by. "What do you need me to do?"

My lips part with a sigh of relief, and I explain my plan to him. I have to promise him tickets to a few performances for his wife before he agrees to my request. Once we disconnect the call, I spend another hour scrolling through Mads' social media.

Enthralled, captivated, impressed; truthfully, none of those words seem to capture just how interesting this woman is. Have I been listening to an episode of her podcast while scrolling? Yes. Still, seeing the amount of research she puts into each episode, post, and how engaged her followers are in what she has to say. How she speaks with authors and readers in a conversational but put together way.

She has me mesmerized, and she doesn't even know.

When I get down to her first post, a promotional picture from my show with a lyric from Marie's character.

Today is my day; you will not keep me away.

I will not be shamed today or any day.

I will make you proud; make me proud before the end of days.

My eyes wide in shock when I read the caption.

The words that saved my life and my sanity are just the beginning of this journey with y'all.

@OPosSideOfSmut:

@OPosSideOfSmut: The words that saved my life and my sanity are just the beginning of this journey with y'all.

The autumn morning air is cool and crisp when I step outside. The leaves covering the streets are bright red and orange already. The scene is breathtaking, and that's just on my street. It's been a while since I've seen the park in fall, well, really, at all. The show has kept me busy, and before I got this role, I was waiting tables in Brooklyn. The hours made it difficult to get to Manhattan during the day.

I pull my jacket tight around me as I begin the trek to the cafe near the park entrance that the carriage rides start. They have hot apple cider, which also just happens to be Mads' favorite fall drink. What? You can't go as far back in a girl's social media as I did last night without finding a hint of her favorite drinks or her favorite snack – Twizzlers – in case you were wondering.

The cafe unlocks its door the same moment I reach for the handle. I step inside to be enveloped in the sweetest mixture of apple and pumpkin scents in the air. I take a moment to look around before I order. My mouth waters when I see a variety of muffins beneath the glass display case. The pumpkin cheesecake looks incredible, but today isn't about me.

"Good morning. How can I help you?" A young woman yawns from behind the counter.

I flash a grin at her and ask for what I came for, plus a few pastries for the carriage ride.

Once my items are packed up, I head back into the cold morning air. I glance across the street, the inside of the park partially hidden by a short stone wall. As I near the meeting spot for the carriages, I hear her voice. My heart skips a beat until the words penetrate my mind.

"You are incredibly handsome." She giggles.

A low growl passes my lips when I step around and see she's petting a horse. I roll my eyes at my ridiculous reaction. Jealous. Of a fucking horse. Jesus, Mary, Joseph and the camel.

I see her before she realizes I'm there. Damn, it's only six forty-five and yet Mads looks like she is ready to walk a runway. I can see the short black skirt that barely covers her ass as I let my gaze track over her gorgeous body. My eyes pause on her creamy thighs which are hidden by sheer black stockings. My dick twitches in my pants. I'd love to wear those thighs as earmuffs. I force my gaze up to see another sweater, this one a burnt orange, which makes her dark eyes pop.

Unable to stay hidden any longer, I step around the large animal.

Mads' voice cracks when she notices me.

"Wh–what are you doing here?"

I had this all planned out. There was going to be a sweet, romantic moment. Unfortunately for me, my brain didn't get the memo.

"I uh– I brought apple cider." I choke on the words.

A middle-aged man climbs into the coachman's seat of the carriage and snorts.

"You were much smoother when you called me last night, kid." The familiar voice chuckles when he takes the reins, nodding for us to take our seats.

Chapter Five

"You are incredibly handsome." I giggle when the massive quadruped, who I've learned is named Ed – yes after the TV show –nuzzles his nose into my neck, which moves my sweater off my shoulder and sends a chill through to my bones. I curse myself for not bringing a jacket. However, in my defense, it's still early November; I wasn't expecting it to be so cold in the morning.

A crackle from somewhere behind me startles me away from the animal, and I glance nervously around my surroundings.

"Nothing to worry about, sweetheart. We should be ready to go in a few minutes." Mr. Phillips, the coachman for my tour today, reassures me when he notices me jumping out of my skin.

I shake my head, amused with myself, and continue to pet the horse's cheek. When I glance up to take in the beauty of the changing leaves, three things happen at the very same time.

One, I take a step toward the carriage ready to take my seat.

Two, I notice someone watching me.

Three, my heart stutters violently in my chest when I see him.

"Wh– what are you doing here?" My voice cracks when I attempt to get the question out.

Dylan's beautiful face drains of color. He looks like he's about to faint. I take a step forward, to do what? I don't know; it's not like I could catch the behemoth of a man if he did in fact fall, but my body moves of its own volition.

"I, uh– I brought apple cider." He stutters; his beautiful blue eyes don't leave my face as he holds a cup out for me to take.

I'm frozen in place when Mr. Phillips chuckles while climbing up into his seat.

"You were much smoother when you called me last night, kid."

Spinning on my heels, I glare at the owner of the tour company.

"I realize now just how creepy this may be; it was meant to be ro-mantic." Dylan rushes out, stumbling over his words. "You– you know, since you– you couldn't go to breakfast with me, I thought I would bring breakfast to you and join you on your tour."

Slowly, I turn to face Dylan, who shrugs as if it makes all the sense in the world. The confidence from yesterday returned. My lungs burn from the breath I'm holding when I finally blow it out. I cross my arms under my chest, raising my large breasts even higher than the push-up bra I'm wearing does. Dylan's gaze drops to my cleavage for a brief second before he lifts his eyes back to mine.

"Is it hot?"

His expression changes to one of confusion instead of embarrassment.

"What?"

"The cider." I roll my eyes at him. "Is the apple cider hot?"

He steps forward, the light slowly returning to his eyes as a gentle smile dances across his lips.

"Yes."

I turn back to the carriage and climb up into my seat.

"Well, come on. I can't let hot cider go to waste."

Dylan's already climbing in behind me before I've finished my sentence. I giggle, unable to hide the amusement. He's kind of adorable when he's nervous.

Mr. Phillips lifts the reins and clicks his tongue at Mr. Ed, indicating it's time to move. Dylan turns to me with an outstretched hand, offering me one of the cups again. This time, I eagerly accept the drink. The sweet scent of warm cinnamon and apple fills my nose when I lift the tab on the lid. My mouth curves up into a warm smile at the thoughtful gesture, though I'm still unsure how he could know about my affinity for hot apple cider. The scent is more pronounced when I lift the cup to my lips and take a cautious sip. A soft appreciative moan escapes when the burst of flavors explode on my tongue.

My God, that is good.

I feel Dylan squirm next to me, and I can't help but turn my gaze to him and smirk with a cocked brow.

"I've lived in New York my entire life. I may be from Brooklyn, but working in the city as much as I do, this is just as much home as where I grew up. And yet, I've never taken a tour like this before." His glance darts around the scenery before it lands back on me. His tone is filled with heat when he continues. "I didn't realize just how beautiful this could be."

The air between us is charged as we stare into each other's eyes. His bright blue irises have me ready to melt into the floor of the carriage. My teeth chatter when another shiver courses through my body. Dylan places his cup between his knees, squeezing the paper cup so it doesn't fall to the ground before he shrugs off his jacket. My eyes drop to his chest and biceps, no longer caring about the chill. His long sleeve thermal fits him like a glove.

How is he so ripped?

I feel his strong arms around me before I realize what he's doing. He hangs his jacket over my shoulders, his warmth invading my space. My cheeks flush at the gesture and how good he smells. My mouth waters at the mixture of the smoky vanilla and woodsy scent, but there's a hint of something else. It reminds me of the gingerbread cookies that Elle makes during the holidays.

When Dylan pulls back, he leaves an arm draped around me, holding the jacket in place. I breathe in the delicious smell of him again before I realize just how close this stranger is to me. And a pretty damn famous stranger at that.

"Why?" I say on a breathy exhale. "How did you know I like cider?"

I feel him stiffen next to me, but he remains a cocoon of warmth around me.

"I felt awful about how Marie treated you." His smooth voice rushes over me like a blanket. "No one deserves that treatment, but especially not you. There's just something about you, Mads."

My mind begins to whirl with his admission. Sure, Marie wasn't nice, but I was invading *their* space. Although Cassie *did* invite me backstage. I shake my head, clearing the thought from my mind.

"When I hung up with Mr. Phillips, I did a deep-dive into your InstaPic account." The words come out in a panic, like he's worried I'll push him out of the moving carriage while he's explaining. "I didn't want to assume you were a fan of pumpkin spice just because it's the season."

My mouth pops open in shock. We sit in silence for a few moments while I let his words sink in; I let out the most ridiculous snort and giggle at both myself and him.

"That is the sweetest and simultaneously creepiest thing anyone has ever done for me." Giggling in response, I continue. "Ironically, I actually live in a town that is best known for its pumpkins and year-round pumpkin spice coffee. I do enjoy it, but not as much as this."

My lips tilt into a sinful smirk as I take another sip of the apple cider.

Dylan lets out a breath, obviously relieved. I shake my head, amused at how this morning has gone. He lifts a white paper bag I didn't see before, with the same cafe name printed on it as the cups.

"I also brought breakfast." His cheeks heat when he hands it over in offering.

Cautiously, I trade my cup for the bag and peek inside. I gasp when I see a box of fresh apple walnut muffins.

"Just how deep did you dive into my post history?" I stare at him, my mouth agape.

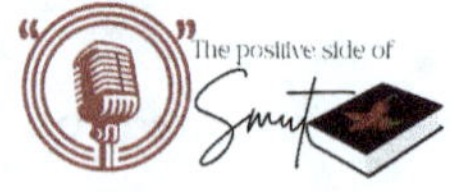

"I'm pretty sure I have a bruise on my ass from climbing up on that statue." I giggle when we step into a restaurant.

Dylan has been with me all day, not leaving my side once. When he told me that they have one day a week where the show doesn't run, and lucky for me, today is that day; I thought that he would leave and do his own thing after.

No, not Dylan. I made one comment about my plan after the tour and as soon as our feet were on the ground after the tour, he took my hand and looped it around his arm, stating he was going with me to check out The Metropolitan Museum of Art. The day has been incredible and memorable, to say the least.

"Thank you for letting me spend the day with you." He whispers the words into my hair, his hand placed confidently on the small of my back as we follow the host to our table.

I glance up at his face, when he helps to slide my chair back under the table after I take a seat. The radiant smile he's got aimed at me sends a flutter in my belly.

"You didn't give me much of a choice." I tease him with a flirtatious wink. "Really though, today was better than I could have imagined on my own."

Our eyes remain locked on one another as he takes the seat across from me. At some point, our server takes our drink orders. I allow Dylan to take charge because he's been talking about this place since he took me to his favorite pizza shop for lunch. The conversation continues as easily as it has all day.

"Tell me more about Ka'Mani." He asks before his lips wrap around the bottle of pale ale.

My face lights up with excitement at the mention of my best friend. I only mentioned being here for her birthday once, for him to remember not only why I'm here, but her name makes my insides melt.

Shit.

I'm screwed.

<h1 style="text-align:center">Chapter Six</h1>

I haven't stopped smiling since Mads allowed me to join her this morning. If I'm honest, I was shocked she didn't fight me when I invited myself to join her at the museum. When we separated after dinner, it took everything in me not to follow her. I don't understand it, but there is a need to protect her like I've never felt before.

The Bergen Street station is quiet when I step off the train. A low growl rumbles from my chest when I pull my phone free from my pocket to find no messages. Mads asked that I not walk her back to her place since we just met. I understand she doesn't know me all that well, but damn, it's been twenty-five minutes and no word on whether she made it back alright.

My lips flatten into a straight line when I reach the exit. The evening air is chilly as I reach the top of the stairs. When I go to pull my jacket tighter around me, I realize I've left it with Mads. I shake my head and chuckle at the realization. A gust of wind sends a shiver through me; I glance up when a rustle sounds overhead to see a mix of orange and red scattered in the trees above. Living in Brooklyn, no one ever realizes just how many trees there are in the city's boroughs.

I groan, giving in to the need to know that Mads is ok. My fingers tap quickly against the screen and send a message.

@DylanBryantOfficial:

> Hey, gorgeous. I just got off my last train. Did you make it back safe?

My face splits into a silly grin when I get a quick response.

@OPosSideOfSmut:

> I just walked in the door.

She sends another message immediately after.

@OPosSideOfSmut:

> There was an altercation on the sidewalk in front of my building, so I had to hover for a bit until they got out of the way.

A fire lights in my veins when I read the second message. I should have walked her home before catching the subway to get home. I tap the video call icon before I can stop myself.

Mads' soft features fill the screen a second later.

"Hey, what's up?" She quirks a brow.

There is a shaky movement as she moves around the room before she makes herself comfortable on her bed, from the look of it.

"Are you ok?" The question comes out in a rush. I glance down just in time to catch sight of a curb. Thankful not to face plant while on a call with her.

She giggles and rolls her eyes at me.

"I'm fine, Dyl, I promise." The warmth in her kind dark eyes, along with the way she shortens my name, has all my blood rushing south. "One of them was caught cheating at the bar down the street. They don't live here; they were just stopped in front of my door."

She shrugs nonchalantly as she explains.

Picking up the pace as the night air becomes even icier, I make it to my front door in record time. Mads notices the relief on my face when I step into the heated apartment. Her beautiful eyes go wide while her cheeks flush.

"Oh shit! I'm still wearing your jacket!"

My lips twist up into a soft smile.

"It's alright, gorgeous. Your comfort is more important than mine." I wink at her through the screen. "Plus, I've got plenty more here."

After kicking off my shoes by the door, I walk through the foyer, crossing the living room to the kitchen.

"What are we doing tomorrow?" I ask as I pull open the refrigerator door and pull out a beer.

Mads shakes her head with a wide smile on her face.

"Who said you were invited?" There is a taunt in her tone that has my mouth popping open in surprise. My reaction only makes her giggle. "I'm kidding. From what I've been reading, it looks like DUMBO is supposed to be pretty fun. And it would be a great place for me to get some pictures for my socials."

She brings her hand to her mouth and worries her bottom lip before she finishes her thought.

"But, I know it's supposed to be a big tourist attraction, so–" Mads' words cut off when I lift the beer to my lips and take a long sip before replying.

"I'll see you in the morning, gorgeous." My lips turn up into a sinful smirk.

Two mornings in a row waking before the sun is extremely uncommon for me. I may have matinees two days a week, but even then it's not necessary for me to be at the theatre until after ten in the morning. My mouth pops open with a yawn so big my jaw pops.

Kinky.

My back is pressed against the bright artwork of the DUMBO wall. A huge attraction that I figured would be an easy thing for Mads to find. Unfortunately, I didn't think it through that I would also be a big draw. I smile down at my phone, rereading the conversation this morning with Mads when I hear someone scream my name.

Fuck.

"Oh, my God! It's Dylan!" one voice yells from a distance.

"Holy shit!" someone else squeals. "It's Dylan Fucking Bryant!"

I raise my gaze to see a group of young women rushing toward me like a swarm. Chuckling nervously, I blow out a deep breath and put on my stage face.

"Fuck! Oh. My. God!" There's a chorus of expletives as they get closer.

"Good morning, ladies."

They're all talking over one another, asking rapid-fire questions I don't have time to answer before the next one comes. I open my mouth ready to answer the first one I can make out when another voice cuts through the chaos.

My gaze darts around the space until it lands on the source. A wide smile spreads across my face, and I push off the wall to close the distance.

Chapter Seven

When a high-pitched sound pierces my eardrums in the morning, I have to all but peel my eyelids open. A frustrated groan passes my lips when I pick up my phone and see the time. Why did I decide to set an alarm for five forty-five in the morning?

A message notification pops up as soon as the annoying sound stops. My lips twitch, unable to fight the smile that spreads.

Once I type out my response, I press send.

I throw my phone down onto the mattress and push myself up. After a quick shower, I get ready faster than I've ever done in the history of my life — I know I should be acting cool, but he's hot and sweet, ok – I grab my phone and request a car from one of the ride share apps.

Unlike yesterday, today I have a jacket – his jacket – and, according to the weather app, it's going to be in the low sixties. By the time I get my shoes on and get down to the front door, my ride is here. Stepping out into the cool morning air, I'm thankful for the extra layer.

The ride to the bridge is filled with comfortable silence. My eyes go wide as we drive through the city streets, and a lightness fills my chest as I take in the beautiful buildings and landscapes I've only ever seen on TV. How is this, my life? Everything about this place is spectacular.

Forty minutes later we're pulling to a stop across from the DUMBO wall Dylan wanted to meet me at. It's far from anything we have at home. Wildly colorful abstract art painted along the brick walls of a building that backs to a park. I step out of the car to see a group of twenty-something women crowding around something, screaming and shrieking. My lips pull up into a wide, sinful smile as I approach.

"Shut the front door! It's THE Dylan Bryant?" I shout, acting like a raging fangirl. "Can I pretty please with a cherry on top have an auto-graph?"

From where I'm standing, I can see the moment Dylan's expression softens when he hears my voice. His eyes dart around all over the place until they land on me. I'm unable to suppress the laugh that builds when he finds me. I don't know that he even bids the women farewell before he leaves them, closing the space between us. My playful smile remains in place when he reaches me until I see the hunger in his eyes.

"Baby, you can have whatever you want."

"Wha–" my words are cut off when he dips down, and his mouth crashes against mine.

Dylan's tongue swipes across the seam of my lips, urging me to part, I gasp in surprise and give him access. My hands fly up to fist the hair at the nape of his neck. All thoughts leave my mind when he swallows the needy moans from me as he explores my mouth with his. I whimper in protest when he pulls away too quickly.

"I–I–uh–well, damn." My hands drop down to my sides when we separate.

"Yeah, I um, I know my momma would want me to apologize for not getting consent before that, but Jesus," he chuckles darkly. "That was one hell of a kiss."

I wave my hand in front of my face, trying to fan myself off. His hands find my hips, and he holds me close while staring into my eyes.

"No." I shake my head, amused that the smile won't quit. "No apology necessary; you can have it retroactively."

With a wicked smile dancing across Dylan's lips, he gently grips my chin between his fingers, leans in and presses a soft kiss against my lips again.

"Are you ready for coffee?"

I nod my head enthusiastically. My thoughts are a woven web of chaos after that exchange. Dylan's hand finds mine, our fingers tangle together, and he guides me out of the park.

My eyes drift up his tall frame, taking in the beauty that is Dylan Bryant. I smile to myself when I realize just how ridiculous this is. Sure, I know I look good; I'm not blind. I'm tall, have a cute face, a killer rack, and a nice ass – the latter of which I one hundred percent attribute to the dance classes. But, I am so not used to this kind of attention.

We walk several blocks, an easy conversation passing between the two of us as has been the case during the time we've spent time together. Dylan is sure to point out things he thinks would interest me or may even be a good post for my InstaPic or SnapTok which he has apparently been stalking when we're apart. That fact warms my heart more than it should be.

"This place has the best coffee and breakfast around here." He squeezes my hand as we come to a stop in front of a small cafe. Tables and chairs are set on the sidewalk on either side of the door.

Stepping inside, I'm hit with an overpowering aroma of freshly brewed coffee. My mouth waters. I'll never admit that out loud to Elle – her blends are out of this world; I'll never deny that. But, they've never had me salivating like someone with a life sentence getting parole.

A sign is posted by the entrance asking that patrons seat themselves, so we make our way to a table in the back corner, away from the crowd. I feel his eyes on me when I read over the many options on the menu. Between coffee, tea, juices ,and so many breakfast options from entrees to pastries, I can't decide.

"Mads, why do you look like you're about to have an aneurysm?" Dylan's smooth voice pulls my attention from the large menu. He reaches across the table, laying his hand on mine.

"How am I supposed to choose? Everything looks amazing!" I shriek with excitement, my free hand flies to cover my mouth when I hear the sound that comes from me. My face heats with embarrassment and a nervous laugh escapes. "Sorry."

"You're good, gorgeous. Which is calling to you most?" He shrugs calmly, "If you could try more than one, what would you choose?"

Not thinking anything of his request, I name off a handful of meals including a sweet chili scramble, avocado bowl, and a pancake platter.

Drool is all but leaking from the corner of my mouth as I recite the food items.

"Christ, you're adorable." Dylan's responding smirk tinges my cheeks a brighter pink.

He excuses himself to go to the counter to order. A few moments later, he returns with a coffee, promising our food will be delivered to the table shortly. My hands wrap around the mug he brought back for me; a soft whimper builds in the back of my throat at the heat of the drink warming my cold skin. I lift the cup to my lips and take a cautious sip. My eyes roll to the back of my head and slowly close while a long, low moan breaks free.

"Obviously, you can't take me anywhere." I drop my face when I respond, my eyes slowly flutter open simultaneously as the food arrives. Every. Single. Thing. I said I wanted to try, is spread across the table. My gaze darts up to see a pleased expression etched across Dylan's face. "What did you do?"

He thanks the server before acknowledging my question.

"You shouldn't have to choose." He lifts my hand he's still holding to his lips. "You won't have to when you're with me, Mads."

My eyes well with unshed tears, a wide smile spreads and I blow out a slow breath. I'm not sure how I've earned this kind of attention or affection, but this man is going to ruin me for anyone else.

When we finish our breakfast a while later, we make our way back outside. He guides me a few blocks toward another mural. Dylan's arm is wrapped around my side when he pulls his phone from his pocket. He stops moving, and his body goes rigid.

I hear a low curse under his breath when he releases me. When I turn to look at him, the blood has drained from his face.

"What's wrong?" I ask in a panic.

He drags a hand through his hair. His eyes are locked on me, but there is still a fear there I just can't figure out.

"Have you ever seen the show Gossip Girl?" He shoves his hands into his pockets.

I snort at the question.

"Like the xoxo Gossip Girl TV show?"

Dylan nods at my question.

"There's someone who runs an InstaPic account with that concept, but for Broadway." He swallows thickly. "And well, pictures of us this morning are on there."

My gaze remains on him, unsure what the big deal is.

"Ok, and?"

He takes my hand, pulling me closer to him.

"Of our kiss." He turns his phone to show me. "I don't want to hide this from you; but the people who follow these things can be brutal, and I don't want you to be blindsided."

I chuckle and shake my head, my eyes refusing to look at the screen.

"No, it's fine; I know you're just being friendly." I smile up at him, trying to be encouraging. "Besides, it's not like anything long term could happen since I'm only here for the week. They'll forget about me soon enough."

Chapter Eight

H er words have been on repeat in my mind like a top forty pop hit since she spoke them this morning.

You're just being friendly. Besides, it's not like anything long term could happen since I'm only here for the week. They'll forget about me soon enough.

What about this is just friendly to her? Especially after that kiss. My cock begins to stiffen at the memory. Fuck. I slide my free hand in my pocket trying to discreetly tuck the growing erection under my waistband.

Besides, it's not like anything long term could happen since I'm only here for the week.

But what if it could? It's only been two days with her, and I can promise you, just this one week will never be enough.

They'll forget about me soon enough.

How could anyone forget about her? Is she just being self-deprecating or does she really believe that? How could I ever forget her?

Mads' voice pulls me out of my thoughts.

"This is it."

We're standing outside of a hookah bar. I glance down at her with an arched brow.

She giggles and shakes her head knowingly while gesturing toward a door partially hidden behind several potted trees.

My lips form a perfect 'o' when I realize the apartment is above the hookah bar.

"Thank you for letting me get you home. I'd have been worried all night." I admit when she types in the access code. "Would you like to come to tonight's show?" I ask, feeling more nervous than I have with her before.

Her dark eyes implore me not to stress over the day's events. I know damn well my emotions are written on my face. I may be a damn good actor on stage, but, fuck me, I can't school my features when it comes to her.

"I am going to see another show tonight." Mads' sweet smile is like a balm to my soul. Something about the serene expression soothes me. "I highly doubt anyone will recognize me if I'm on my own." She giggles.

"Baby, you're unforgettable. That's why I haven't been able to say goodbye." I admit quietly while stepping into her space as she opens the door. My arms wrap tightly around her curvaceous figure as I lean in to kiss her forehead this time. She trembles in my arms at the tender connection.

I suck in a deep breath, filling my lungs with the warm late afternoon air. Unable to release my hold on her, I rest my chin on top of her hair.

"The next matinee is tomorrow, so I won't be able to see you in the morning." The words are a strained whisper.

"That's ok, there's actually somewhere I've been wanting to go on my own so that will work out well!" She is way too eager.

Instead of asking the obvious of what she's wanting to do on her own, I try again to secure a time I'll get to see her.

"How about the performance tomorrow night?"

She nods her head enthusiastically.

"I'll be there." She leans into me, her arms snake around my middle, her head lies against my chest and she holds me tight against her.

"Gorgeous?" I pause until she glances up at me. When she finally does, I continue. "What do you want to do on your own?"

Mads leans back, her eyes boring into mine. She has the most seductive confident air about her right now. I swallow thickly while I wait for her response.

"The Museum of Sex." She smirks at me and winks before turning on her heel and walking up the stairs to her rental

I step offstage at the end of the night. I got here with just enough time to get ready, so I haven't had the chance to catch up with anyone. Although my mind has been stuck on a certain feisty raven-haired beauty even during my performance.

"D!" Annie's voice startles me out of thoughts of my day with Mads.

I glance around to find her rushing up behind me.

"Hey, what's up?" I pause in place.

When she catches up with me, we fall into step together. We walk in silence toward my dressing room for less than a minute before she nudges me with her elbow.

"Soooooo," the one word is elongated and sing-songy.

I chuckle and shake my head at her.

"What?"

"Ugh!" she groans. "You're such a guy. We haven't talked since Sunday night. Did you get in touch with Maddox?"

I drag a hand through my hair and lead her into the private space. Grabbing my phone from the storage drawer, I glance up at her.

"I take it you haven't seen it?" My fingers tap the screen as I pull up the post from @BetweenTheLines. There are two pictures featured in the carousel; the first is the kiss, and God damn, the way her body responded to me when I dipped her during the connection was incredible. The second picture is of the two of us staring into each other's eyes after. A caption underneath which says *@DylanBryantOfficial spotted with an unknown woman in DUMBO early this morning. Who is this mystery girl? Don't worry, Besties. I will dig for answers. xoxo Broadway*

Annie gasps beside me. Her nails dig into my forearm and pull me to a stop. When she releases my arm, she immediately smacks my chest.

"You motherfucker!" The words come out as a shriek. "She is too good for you! But– I'm not gonna lie, you look so good together!"

"We really do." I roll my eyes. "But we're just friends. That kiss was just..." I peel off the shirt portion of my costume and toss it to the side, allowing the cool room air to dry the sweat from my skin.

"It was what?"

"She showed up and sarcastically fan-girled over me when she saw a group of women surrounding me this morning." I explain, my lips twitch up into a smirk. "There was just something about the way she spoke and how she rescued me that I couldn't help myself."

I fall back, landing on the small puke-green couch in my room. It's hideous, but comfortable. Annie kicks off her shoes and sits on the arm of the couch with her feet resting on the cushions.

"Oh bro! You are so boned!" she giggles, clapping her hands together and kicking her feet like a maniac toddler who had sugar for the first time. "So, when are you going to see her again?"

I glance at the picture again, tapping the screen a few more times before I go into the messages I've shared with Mads.

@DylanBryantOfficial:

Sweet dreams, gorgeous.

I shove my phone back into my pocket; my eyes drift up to Annie.

"She's coming to tomorrow night's performance." I say quietly when I hear Marie stomping around in the hallway.

Chapter Nine

P olice sirens nearby assault my ear drums, tearing me from a peaceful sleep. I open my eyes and see red and blue lights flashing on the walls, shining through the small window. My eyes are now wide open, darting around the room as I bolt upright. My hand flies to my chest as if it can hold my racing heart in place. I glance at the time to see it's only five in the morning.

"Definitely not in Kansas anymore." I say through a yawn while I scrub the sleep from my eyes.

Most mornings in Hollow Heights I'm greeted by a chorus of birds singing, so this is a vast difference than what I'm used to. I swing my legs over the side of the bed to stand, allowing myself a moment to stretch the soreness from my muscles. Is it just me, or is there something about not being in your own bed that kills your body?

After several moments of staring blankly into the void, reluctantly I stand and make my way to the bathroom so I can get ready for the day. A shiver rushes over my body when my feet hit the cold tile floor of the shower, so I reach in to turn on the water and allow it to warm up. My nipples pebble as I drag my oversized T-shirt over my head and the chill of the morning air caresses my bare skin. I step into the shower, pleasantly surprised by the strong pulsing water pressure, and I sigh softly as the high heat cascades down to my pale skin. My mind wanders as the memory of yesterday's events plays back.

The feel of Dylan's lips on mine echoes through my thoughts; and a rush of desire spreads to my core. Heat and arousal pool between my thighs from just the ghostly presence of that kiss. I close my eyes and press my hands against the cool tile wall, trying to clear my mind, which doesn't seem to work. When I allow my eyelids to flutter open, I glance up at where the water is streaming from; my lips dance into a wicked grin as I take in the removable showerhead.

The hose attachment moves easily enough, and after glancing at the settings, I twist the lever at the head. Once the pressure is constant, I lower it between my thighs.

"Oh, fuck!" I gasp when the stream hits my clit for the first time and toss my head back, enjoying the sensation on the sensitive peak. My hips buck into the force of the water and my body demands more. I cup my breast with my free hand, paying special attention to my nipple. A soft whimper escapes my lips as the delicious feelings of an impending orgasm begins to build. I allow my mind to wander to what it would feel like to have Dylan's hands on my body. The moment I allow myself to give into the desire of being with him, I fall over the edge.

"Oh my god." I cry out into the empty room. After a moment of silence passes, I giggle at myself.

I am so screwed.

An hour later, I find myself strolling through Central Park with a hot cup of coffee in hand. My lips turn up into a warm smile as I take in the beautiful green landscape. I may have been here once before, but I was a little too distracted to pay much attention to my surroundings. The cityscapes over these past few days have been a huge change to my surroundings back home. I'm so used to farmland after living in Hollow Heights all my life with the exception of a few years at the University of Illinois, though—Ka'Mani and I spent most of our time at the library or in our dorm binge watching episodes of Mob Wives.

I drag my fingers through my long dark hair while my thoughts drift to the last time I was here. I smirk to myself and head toward the Alice in Wonderland statue that Dylan took me to before. As soon as I arrive, I grab my phone from the pocket of his jacket that I have yet to give back and snap a selfie of myself smiling in front of the statue with the beautiful pastel colors of the sunrise peeking through the background.

Before I put the device away, I open the message he sent me last night and attach the picture along with a response.

@OPosSideOfSmut:

> Woke up ridiculously early and had to come to my new favorite place.

His response comes much faster than I expected for this hour.

@DylanBryantOfficial:

> Well, now I have a third contender for my favorite picture of you.

My brow arches while I read his response.

What are the other two options?

The pictures he sends me has my jaw dropping. I lose my grip on the coffee, which falls to the ground. Somehow it lands right-side up and doesn't explode or splash on me. There's no way I'm looking at what I think I'm looking at. My brain has to be creating its own hopeful narrative.

My eyes are locked on a picture of us in front of the DUMBO wall. He has me in a deep dip, our mouths locked together in a passionate kiss. I swallow thickly as I take in the image before scrolling to the next, one of us staring into one another's eyes like we're the only two people in the world. Seeing the image that played through my mind while I made myself come this morning makes my cheeks heat. On the flip side of that, the way we're staring at one another in that second picture has a breath stuck in my chest.

I'm partial to the last one.

I step out of the museum after spending several hours thoroughly touring each exhibit and lean with my back against the cool brick wall to finish writing up the notes for what I want to talk about either in today's social media post or an upcoming podcast. My phone vibrates in my pocket. I smirk when I pull the device out to see a few messages from Dylan.

I can't wait to see you tonight. I've been spoiled the past few mornings with you.

Just stepped off stage, come by early if you want. We can have dinner here before tonight's show.

A warmth fills my chest reading the words on my screen. He's annoyingly sweet, and yet, I can't get enough of it. I type the address for the theatre in my phone's GPS and can't help the goofy grin that spreads across my face when I see it's a short walk from where I am.

I'm not too far away; see you in ten!

Shockingly, I get to every intersection when the pedestrian crossing light turns to walk and make it in less than the estimated time. I approach the stage door just as it slowly opens, inch by inch until Cassie's face emerges from the darkness inside.

"Hey girl, come on before anyone sees us!" She waves, urging me to move fast.

Once I'm inside with her, she loops her arm around mine and guides me through the halls.

"So how are you and Dylan getting along?" She nudges my side.

My lips curve up into a smile.

"Pretty good." Unsure just how much to admit, I prefer to keep the details close to my chest until I know what he is thinking because, I mean, I'm going back to Hollow Heights in a few days.

Cassie leads me to a room with the door open. I see Dylan sitting with his back to the door, Annie sitting across from him on an ugly green couch.

"I think if that's the last kiss I get in my life, I will die happy. But Jesus Christ, Annie. What I would give to have another one." He groans and sucks in a breath before he continues. Annie's eyes lock on mine; a wicked glint shines bright while she listens. "Everything about the way Mads feels in my arms, and–" he half moans and growls – "her lips taste like an orange creamsicle."

Chapter Ten

Cassie giggles and walks into the room with a hand over her mouth to hide a smile. There is a sinful smirk on my lips when Dylan slowly turns around in his chair and his cool eyes find me standing there waiting for him. They go wide as he takes me in, leaning against the door frame with a hand propped on my hip. His mouth pops open like he's about to speak, but I wave my hand at him, dismissing whatever he's about to say.

"That retroactive consent was also for any future exchanges as well." I wink at him.

Dylan turns back to face Annie, who is laughing so hard tears are streaming down her cheeks.

"Well, I'm sure as hell not going to kiss you." She catches her breath long enough to taunt him through another throaty laugh.

Without another word passing his lips, Dylan quickly stands and stalks toward me like a lion about to pounce. He crosses the distance in a single beat. The second he reaches me, his mouth crashes against mine. His hands cup my face to hold me in place. My lips part as I let out a gasp when he presses his hips against me, allowing me to feel his generous length through his pants. Dylan doesn't waste the opportunity I've given him and slides his tongue inside. He devours and explores everything he can. I moan into the kiss when he gently sucks on my tongue. The skin near my lips smarts where it hadn't before. I raise my arms, wrapping them around his neck, enjoying the sensual moment and forgetting our surroundings. The kiss slows after a few moments, and he pulls away but not before nipping my bottom lip.

"Hi, gorgeous." He presses his forehead against mine. Both of our chests heaving as we try to relearn how to breathe.

"Hi." I whimper into the small space between us and raise my gaze to look at him. His previously bare sharp jawline is now covered with a scruff of hair, like he hasn't shaved today which explains the sting. I cautiously rake my fingers through the short hair and smirk up at him.

"I like this."

A throat clears from inside what I presume is a dressing room.

"Goddamn, that was hot." Annie is fanning herself with a notebook.

Cassie thwacks her arm and shakes her head.

"Perv."

"Alright – I love you both, but go away." Dylan's arm snakes around my waist, guiding me into the private space.

The two women wiggle their fingers at us as they leave, closing the door behind them. Meanwhile, he drags me to the couch Annie was sitting on just a minute earlier. He takes a seat before immediately pulling me down next to him. I'm so close I'm nearly on his lap. My cheeks heat at the dirty image that appears in my mind at the thought of being on top of him.

"Fuck, it's good to see you," Dylan breathes into my hair. "How was your morning?"

I pull my legs underneath me and lean against him while I tell him about the museum. The only time he makes an inappropriate joke is when I bring up the bounce house made of boobs, which honestly – I can't blame him. It was an entertaining experience. Our conversations continue to flow easily, even when there is a break; the silence is comfortable. It's over an hour later when my stomach growls and I realize I haven't eaten since having a muffin at breakfast.

Dylan grabs his phone from the table in front of us, where it's been sitting face down this entire time. I pull mine from my bag sitting in front of me on the floor and check my messages when I see one from Ka'mani. Before I have a chance to read or reply to it his voice drags my attention from the device.

"Dinner will be here in a few minutes. There's a great burger place around the corner, so she shouldn't be long." I arch a brow at him in question, and he chuckles, "I offered to buy the girls' dinner if they went to pick it up for us."

His phone is back on the table in front of us; however, this time it's facing up. I squeak in surprise when I recognize the image on his lock screen. Words are stuck in my throat when I point at the phone, my eyes locked on him. Dylan's face tinges pink, unable to meet my gaze as he drags his fingers through his hair.

"I wasn't lying when I said I couldn't decide on my favorite picture." He unlocks the device before handing it to me, revealing another familiar image and shrugging.

My heart pounds hard in my chest as I allow the knowledge that he has the two pictures of us someone sent to a gossip account as his lock and home screen.

I stare with my mouth agape, still in shock, unsure if he's giving Joe Goldberg or golden retriever energy. My gut tells me it's the latter. Before I can talk myself out of it, I rise so I'm kneeling on the couch next to him. Dylan's eyes are light with a knowing smile, and I lean in. The door to the room opens at the same moment. Annie and Cassie walk in with a few brown paper-bags and bottles of water.

"Shit, our bad." Cassie covers her face with one of the bags.

I sit back down next to him, my lips twitch into a shy grin, and I shake my head.

"Shoot, I'll watch." Annie waggles her brows before taking a seat in the armchair Dylan was sitting in when I first arrived.

A strangled groan leaves the man sitting next to me. I snort, unable to hide my amusement at his frustration. So sexy, I know.

"Sooooo," Annie lets out in a singsong tone. "Mads, how long are you going to be here?"

Confusion must be apparent on my face because she continues quickly.

"It's just that we have so many questions." There is a hopeful smile dancing on her lips as she explains.

"We?" Dylan responds before I have a chance to.

As soon as the question is out of his mouth, three more people crowd into the confined space. I fight back the emotion when I see they all have copies of the newest release by an author I had on my podcast last week.

"I'm staying for tonight's performance, so you have me until you have to be on stage."

The next few hours go by in a flash. Being able to have such personal conversations with readers face to face about how smut and romance novels in general have changed their lives and relationships for the better is unlike anything I've experienced before. I expected Dylan to leave when the juicier bits of the books I read and interviews I've conducted come up, but he never leaves my side. If anything, he just pulls me in closer as if he's staking his claim. Truth be told, if I'm already getting this attached, the end of the week is going to be hell.

Chapter Eleven

M arie is center stage singing one of the most popular numbers from the show. Most nights I stand here, just offstage, tapping my foot along with the beat. The song is catchy, and there is no denying Marie's talent, but she's always rubbed me the wrong way.

Tonight though – tonight, while I'm listening for my cue to enter stage left, my gaze is locked on the woman in the fifth row near the aisle, closest to the stage access door.

Mads' eyes shine with emotion while she watches intently. There is a lightness in the way she's staring intently at Marie as if she's in awe of the woman, or at least the character.

It's nearly impossible to keep my eyes focused on Marie during the final scene we have together. When I call out for *Monica's* hand, Marie turns to me. The character is supposed to be celebrating her big win before the finale, yet her stare is laser focused on me. She has a terrifying expression etched across her usually soft features in this scene as if she's ready to barrel through me. Miraculously, I hit my mark and recite the lines without fumbling.

Precisely six minutes and thirty seconds later, yes, we've timed it – the entire cast is on stage for the curtain call. I take my place between Marie and Annie for our bow and then rush off the stage. Today I'm more thankful than most that there is a small shower in my dressing room. I make my way back to the private space to clean the sweat and proof of tonight's performance from my body.

After a record-breaking quick shower, I step out, wrapping a large white towel around my waist. Beads of water drip down my bare chest while I grab the clothes I stuffed in my backpack. A cool breeze caresses my back, sending a shiver through my body. I turn to see Cassie and Mads standing in the open doorway. A dramatic gagging noise comes from Cassie, who quickly averts her eyes and runs back out of the room, closing the door behind her, while Mads' gaze never leaves my chest.

"Hey, gorgeous," I fight the urge to laugh and wave my hand toward my face, "my eyes are up here."

Her cheeks flush a beautiful shade of pink.

"I'm not sorry; you're on full display right now. How's a girl not supposed to look?" Mads fans herself, her eyes remain focused on my bare skin until I drag a thermal over my head and cover myself. The moment her focus is broken, I saunter toward her with a sinful smile dancing across my lips. My mouth crashes against hers, and she melts into the kiss that doesn't last nearly long enough before there is a knock on the door. I pull away with a frustrated groan, pressing my forehead against hers and call out to whomever is on the other side.

"What do you want?"

Cassie opens the door again with her hand over her eyes.

"A few of us are going out for drinks if you two want to join us."

I cock a brow at Mads who is smirking up at me with a taunting expression.

"Not tonight. I'll see y'all tomorrow, Cassie."

Our fingers are tangled together as Mads and I step out onto the sidewalk, which is surprisingly empty for this time of night. We walk in silence toward her place when I feel her eyes on me. I glance down to see she's nibbling her bottom lip nervously.

"What is it?" My voice is low as I squeeze her hand reassuringly.

There is another moment of silence that passes between us before she finally speaks up.

"I'm curious." Mads voice is soft as she speaks, "You're still interested in spending time with me after getting a glimpse of what I do?"

Her cheeks heat under my gaze, and my jacket that she's still wearing is open just enough to see that her chest is a beautiful shade of red as well. I pause, pulling her to a stop, slowly encroaching on her space until her back is pressed against the side of the building. My palms are pressed flat against the rough brick on either side of her head, caging her in.

"Is this a serious question?" I drag my nose up the side of her neck, inhaling the sweet mixture of orchids and warm honey. Mads shivers against me and lets out a soft whimper in response. "My gorgeous Habanero-"

"Wait, what?" Mads interrupts and pulls back a fraction.

"You're as spicy as the books you read, gorgeous, and it's my favorite pepper."

Mads gasps in response to my explanation which gives me an in to get closer to her again to finish my thought.

"I have never met someone who exudes so much confidence in what they do, Habanero." I shake my head and chuckle; the short facial hair grazes her delicate skin before I press my mouth against the flesh behind her ear. "There has never been a moment in my life where I have felt such an overwhelming possessive need to claim another person, the way my entire being craved to announce to anyone who was listening that you're mine this afternoon. I had to adjust myself more than once just listening to the excitement in your voice as you spoke about what you're passionate about."

Without giving her a chance to respond, I crush my mouth against hers. She responds with the most sensual moan, and I answer it by pressing my hard length against her stomach so she can feel what she does to me. Mads' hands wrap around my waist urging me to continue but I pull back, panting. There is no way in hell I'm going to let anyone else experience the noises she makes for me.

I pull her close, my hand pressing firmly against the small of her back as we walk the last block to her place. My brow arches when I watch Mads type in the code for the building. It's the date she arrived. I inwardly cringe knowing that's not as impregnable as I'd expect a secured building to be.

Mads turns to face me, her eyes full of lust, as she nods her head toward the door, silently asking me to come in. A sinful smirk spreads across her face when I step inside to follow her. The third-floor walkup gives me an unforgettable view, which only seems to feed the desire that has been building in me since the first time I saw her. Mads' hips sway in a hypnotic rhythm with every step, sending my thoughts through so many scenarios of what I can do with her, to her. By the time we reach her door, my dick is straining against the denim fabric of my jeans. I can feel the zipper digging into the velvety skin.

No sooner than we get inside her space, I am on her. My lips crush against hers and I back her against the closed door. My fingers dig into her luscious hips as I grind my stiff cock against her stomach again. She lets out a breathy gasp; her hands fly up to grab my hair and take hold to deepen the kiss. I groan into her mouth while we explore one another. She reaches between us, making quick work of unbuttoning my jeans. I step back, separating myself from a kiss that could go on forever, and grin down at her.

"Mads, we have all night." I say through a panting breath.

She winks up at me and drops to her knees, her perfectly manicured fingers hooking under the denim and boxer brief waistbands along my waist, tugging them down over my hips. A low groan rises from my chest when my cock springs free. Her pink tongue darts out, wetting her lips before she makes a confession that has me ready to blow.

"And I've been dreaming of what you taste like since that first morning, let me find out." She leans in so close I can feel the puff of warm air rush over my crown when she lets out a plea, begging so beautifully that denying her is no longer an option, "please." She begs.

The ability to form cohesive thoughts escapes me when her warm mouth envelopes the head. My mouth pops open as I suck in a sharp breath. Her tongue swirls sensually around the tip before she takes me deeper.

"FUUCCKK" The word comes out in a low growl while I ball one hand in a fist. I try to think of anything other than the woman on her knees in front of me so I don't blow my load like a two-pump chump. I cup her face, gently caressing her soft skin with my thumb while I allow my gaze to briefly drop to her just as she hollows her cheeks and takes me so deep I feel the back of her throat.

"Mads," her name comes out somewhere between a moan and a pant, "you are fucking perfect."

She whimpers in response to my words before she releases me. I reach down to pull her up, but she grips onto my thigh with one hand. I realize the other is in her pants. Has she been touching herself this entire time? Oh, fuck me.

"I have fucked myself so many times the past few nights fantasizing about how you would fuck my face and finally allow me to taste your cum." Her confession has my dick throbbing with need.

Knowing she has me at her mercy, she takes my cock back in her mouth. My eyes close while I enjoy the unbelievable feel of her mouth on me. Mads' words repeat in my mind. She's fantasized about me fucking her face? Jesus Christ, perfect isn't a strong enough word. My lips pull up into a wicked grin, and my eyes drift down to lock with hers. I drag my fingers through her long black hair and pull it off her face. I test her sincerity by gently thrusting my hips, forcing myself further into her mouth. The moan she lets out around my cock has me ready to explode.

"Tap my thigh twice if you need me to stop." I announce.

She stares up at me, her mouth full, and her eyes shine with excitement. I begin to slowly pump into her, her nails digging into my flesh as she whimpers around me. The vibration of her noises around my cock have me ready to explode. Unable to hold back anymore, I take her, exactly as requested. Her hair is still wrapped around my fist while I hold her head steady and use her for my own pleasure. It doesn't take long before I unload, filling her mouth. She swallows around me as she takes in every drop I release.

"Fuck me, I'm never going to have enough of you." I admit as I step back when she releases me. Her hand is still between her legs.

I pull her up to her feet; she lets out a frustrated whine. My lips are on hers in a second. Tasting myself on her tongue has my cock already coming back to life. I shove my jeans the rest of the way off and kick them to the side. As soon as I'm free, I make quick work of removing her pants and panties. My hands are on her bare hips while my mouth is still on hers, and I guide us backward until my calves hit the bed.

I drag my shirt over my head as soon as I sit down. A desperate need to feel her bare skin against mine, I reach for hers and slowly expose her creamy flesh. Her cheeks flush when my gaze drifts back up to her face.

"It's my turn." I lean in, pressing my mouth against hers one last time. "You're not the only one who has been fantasizing. Right now, you're going to ride my face and let me get my fill of you."

"What? No!" Mads' desire that was there a second ago is now hidden behind a frantic reaction. "I'm too big. I'll hurt you!"

I let out a snort and lift her onto the bed without much effort, carefully lowering her onto my stomach as I lay back onto my elbows.

"No, you won't. But even if you did," I squeeze her hips, massaging the pliant flesh. "What a good fucking way to go."

She groans at the feel of my hands on her.

"Give me what I want, gorgeous."

Chapter Twelve

Last night's events replay in my mind as I step out of the bathroom, pulling on the last of my clothes. I glance over at Mads, who is still sprawled across the bed fast asleep, and I can't help the smile that forms. I've never woken up so energized, especially after so little sleep, but something about the way she took my cock after I made her come several times with my tongue and fingers — she was insatiable — and fuck me, it was incredible.

I get a notification on my phone from a food delivery app and quietly rush out of the room to head downstairs. While I wait inside the door, I notice that there is a new post from @BetweenTheLines. I tap on the profile and see another picture of Mads and I from yesterday before the show. We're kissing in my dressing room. Someone snapped a picture before Annie and Cassie gave us privacy. I can see their profiles in the picture's background.

The caption, though, is what pisses me off. Usually, this person doesn't come after someone like this. Sure there are trolls that show up in the comment sections, but it's never been the person running the account.

@BetweenTheLines: @DylanBryantOfficial seen in an intimate moment with a plus-size nobody. Who is this stranger? Has she really taken fan favorite Dylan Bryant off the market? Stay tuned to find out! xoxo Broadway.

@BetweenTheLines: @DylanBryantOfficial seen in an intimate moment with a plus-size nobody. Who is this stranger? Has she really taken fan favorite Dylan Bryant off the market? Stay tuned to find out!
xoxo Broadway.

There is a soft knock against the thick door separating me from the outside elements. I quickly thank the person and take my order without making eye contact. My vision has already blurred into a red haze after seeing the post about Mads and me. It doesn't help that comments have started rolling in with trash talk about her as a person because they are jealous of how close she is to me when they'll never get that chance.

I carefully balance the two steaming cups in one hand while re-adjusting the bag of food. Anger rolls through me in waves as I take the stairs two at a time to get back to her. I hope she hasn't woken up yet. When I step back into the room where I left Mads, I find her sitting up; her face resting in her hands.

A soreness I haven't felt in ages has consumed every muscle and bone of my body. Even in my toes, I didn't realize toe-curling orgasms really were a thing until last night. I reach around the bed for Dylan, hoping for a repeat this morning. Knowing that I'll only have him for a few more days makes me want to spend the rest of my time in NYC in bed. My eyelids flutter open when I feel nothing but cold sheets. I sit up and glance around the small space. He's gone. His clothes are gone. I drop my face into my hands and let out a frustrated groan.

We aren't anything serious; it was just fun. I shouldn't have expected him to stay the entire night. I remind myself.

My body goes rigid when I hear a soft click, thankful the sheet is still covering my bare body.

"Good morning, Habanero."

I jerk my gaze up to find Dylan standing at the door with two to-go cups and a white paper bag with a smiley face and the words *Bon Appétit* stamped on the side.

"What? Hi. What?" I scrub my hands against my tired eyes. "What's going on?"

He chuckles and crosses the space in one long step before taking a seat on the bed next to me. There's an emotion in his eyes I can't quite place when his mouth brushes lightly against mine.

"I had to run down to get the food I ordered." His lips tug at the corner with a knowing smirk when he hands me a cup. "I figured the apple cider wouldn't do it today."

My brow arches, silently questioning what he's up to when I take a sip and my eyes go wide. A concoction of coffee, apple, and toasted walnuts explodes on my taste buds.

"What is this?" I exclaim and quickly take another sip.

He leans in, pressing his lips against the sensitive skin behind my ear, sucking gently before he whispers his response.

"Breakfast."

My body shakes with laughter at his sarcastic response.

"Well, thank you." I hesitate when he sits back up; his bright eyes remain on me while I hold the drink to my mouth. Deciding to be vulnerable and honest is hard, but it's gotten me this far. I suck in a deep breath and let out a confession that makes me feel weak. "I thought I scared you away."

He shakes his head, but there's a sadness in his eyes.

"Not a chance, but there is something that may scare you away."

I stare into his hypnotic blue eyes, curious what could possibly scare me away.

"What's wrong?"

Dylan taps the screen of his phone before handing it over to show me the most recent post from the *Gossip Girl* wannabe.

I snort when I see *plus-size nobody*. The comments are a little harsh, but people can be assholes. I know who I am, and really, that's all that matters.

"They're not wrong. As far as this world is concerned, I am a nobody."

He growls angrily and snatches the phone back.

"It's bullshit. They have no right to make those posts. I'm messaging them."

There's a sinking feeling in my stomach as I watch him. He's the first person I've slept with since working on myself and confidence, both in and out of the bedroom. I glance down at my lap before I speak.

"Well, I mean– if you don't want your fans knowing you're spending time with me, I can just remove myself from the equation." I raise my shoulders and drop them as nonchalantly as I can. Acting as if the offer doesn't break a piece of me is harder than I'd expect.

Dylan's furious gaze drifts away from his phone and back to me. When he sees my face, his expression softens.

"What?" He tucks his finger under my chin, forcing me to look at him. "My sweet Habanero, I am more than ok with everyone knowing you're mine. I don't like how they're referring to you."

I choke on a laugh.

"Ok, superstar." I roll my eyes, but a smile spreads across my face. "Calling me a plus-size nobody is probably the nicest way they can and will refer to me."

His eyes darken while I speak.

"I'm used to being the fat girl." I shrug again and blow out a breath. "Sure, it isn't the best feeling, but I've been called so much worse, so it is what it is."

I wrap my free hand that's not holding my coffee around his when something about his previous statement clicks into place.

"Wait," I blink several times, repeating his words over and over in my mind. "What do you mean, yours?"

My heart stutters when Dylan's tongue darts out, wetting his lips before he presses his mouth against mine. The kiss lasts nowhere near long enough. I let out a needy whine when he's gone.

"I've been trying to figure out how I was going to say goodbye to you after a week of just being in your presence." He chuckles, "but, after last night, if you think there is any way in hell I'm giving you up, you are sorely mistaken."

Emotion swells inside me at his confession; a wave of relief washes over me knowing it isn't one-sided. I rise to my knees, tossing a leg on the other side of his hip to straddle him and wrap my arms around his neck. We get lost in another kiss, his phone long forgotten somewhere on the mattress. The feel of his hands on my bare skin elicits sinful memories from the night before, sending a rush of heat between my thighs.

I grind my bare pussy against the denim fabric that separates us; a soft moan rises from my chest when the friction hits just right on my clit. There's a need between us that neither can deny. Dylan lifts me off him and tosses me onto the bed. He stands, making quick work of removing his clothes.

He stands in front of me; his body chiseled to perfection from his rigid training and performance schedule. My eyes rake up and down his frame, taking in every ridge and valley that make up the delicious man before me. A deep chuckle pulls my attention back to his face.

"Gorgeous, if you keep looking at me like that, I'm going to blow my load on your tits before I get a chance to feel you come around my cock again."

My core tightens at his words.

"That would be a waste when I'm already drenched." I giggle.

Dylan's eyes light with excitement; they never leave mine while he lifts his hand between us, twirling his index finger in a circle. A rush of excitement runs through me as I dutifully obey his request and turn my back to him. I feel the warmth of his body as he inches closer.

His large hand caresses my neck before he presses firmly on my shoulders, urging me to lay my face on the bed; the other has a strong grip on my hip. I feel a shiver of anticipation when the blunt head of his cock presses against my entrance.

"Dylan," his name passes my lips as a whispered plea. "I need you."

A guttural groan rises from deep in his chest; I try to move to take what I want, which is impossible from this position. His fingers dig into my flesh, forcing me to stay still. I'm startled when he removes his right hand and brings it down fast and hard against my ass. The sting of his slap does nothing to stop the yearning that's building in me.

"So needy."

My response is cut off when he presses inside me.

"Fuck," I gasp, "yes!"

There's a beat where Dylan goes still, allowing me to get used to his size just like last night. Being the brat that I am, I push back, taking him as deep as he can go. I cry out with pleasure when I feel him jut into me.

"Mads, I need you to give me a minute." He pants out through gritted teeth.

I let out a whimper, not wanting to wait. Knowing my body and how good he feels, if I have the right amount of pressure, I'm not going to last either. I reach for the bedside table and grab the bright neon pink wand he used on me at some point last night.

"Dyl," I rush out as I fumble with the toy and position it against my clit, "I want you to fuck me so hard and fast the headboard leaves a dent in the wall. Because as soon as I turn this on, I'm going to be the one not lasting long."

"FUUUCKKK" he growls out and thrusts into me hard. I squeak in surprise when he doesn't give me a warning, which turns into a long moan when he finds his rhythm.

I click on the toy, and the constant vibration against the sensitive bundle of nerves feels like a new kind of high. Between that and the way he takes me harder and hits the exquisite spot inside me, the more forceful the headboard crashes against the wall.

I feel the telltale signs that my climax is nearing just as his dick seems to swell inside me. We may not be using protection after a lengthy conversation last night of just how long it's been for both of us, and even though I'm on birth control, I don't want him to come inside me this morning. I click up the intensity of the vibrator.

"Mark me. Come on my tits, like you said. Fuck. Please." The words come out a jumbled mess as I cry out, my pussy convulsing around his thick length.

"Jesus Christ." Dylan growls so low I barely hear him before he's gone, and I suddenly feel so empty. The wand is still buzzing away on my clit when his hands land on my sides, rolling me onto my back. He straddles my stomach, and with a hand wrapped firmly around himself he strokes his velvety skin until ropes of hot cum rush from him onto my skin. His head lulls back between his shoulders as he revels in the bliss of finding his release. I practically sob when another orgasm rolls through me as I see him lose control over me like this.

My God, I never want to get out of this bed.

Chapter Thirteen

Excitement fills my chest when I see the pink exterior of a bookstore I've been excited to visit. After Ka'mani found it during her weekend adventures with local friends, she hasn't stopped talking about the little shop. My plan was to come by earlier in the week; however, I've been distracted. Although I don't think anyone could fault me for that.

My lips pull up into a wide smile when memories of the past forty-eight hours come rushing back. Knowing he's working on pre-scheduled press and media for the show makes the fact that I'm leaving tomorrow afternoon that much more depressing.

I pull out my phone and record a quick video of the outside and the experience of stepping inside before turning the device off. My lips part with a gasp when I see how perfectly the shop is decorated. Old books are hung on the open space of the walls in place of paint or wallpaper. Rolling ladders are connected to two long bookshelves, and there is a cute reading nook with bright pink chairs.

"Wow," I breathe as I take in the space.

"Hi, welcome to The Shredded Bodice!" A feminine voice calls from the back of the shop. "I'll be out in just one second!"

My eyes roam over the inventory. So many beautiful titles line the shelves. A genuine bright smile spreads across my face when I notice a few of my favorite indie authors. I reach out to grab the newest release from Aoife Rye. She's wildly talented and one of the sweetest authors I've had the pleasure of getting to know during the time I've been producing my podcast, *"O" — The Positive Side of Smut.*

The person who welcomed me a few minutes ago makes their appearance when I end up in front of the local authors section, which is surprisingly large. My eyes go wide when I see that my friend Fallon's favorite author, K.D. Smalls, books are all here. I didn't realize she was New York-based.

"Hi!" I walk over to the counter and put down the armful of books I picked up. I obviously had to pick up the signed copies of K.D.'s for Fallon. A middle-aged woman with mousy brown hair styled in a long braid hanging over her shoulder stands behind the counter. She's wearing the cutest pink cable-knit sweater dress I've ever seen.

"Hi there, I'm so sorry for the wait. My name is Enid. Is there anything I can help you with, or are you just browsing today?" She chuckles when she sees the growing pile.

Laughter erupts from my chest as I add the last book in Nikki Grant's Mocha and Makeup series.

"Honestly, I shouldn't be browsing at all since I have to get the train tomorrow to head home, but my friend told me about this place, and I would be doing a disservice to myself if I didn't stop by." I snort and grab another book from a nearby shelf. "Do you mind if I record a video for my social media? I can keep you out of it if you'd prefer."

Enid agrees and even offers to record it for me so I can do an on-camera tour. We get through filming it in less than ten minutes. I talk fast; it's the Gilmore in me. What? Just because I'm a book addict doesn't mean I don't have a guilty pleasure TV show or two. The two of us are giggling like old friends by the time we're done and head back to the counter where I put the last of my books. In my defense, at least five of the–listen, the number of books I'm buying isn't important; what is, is that some are for other people.

"This is going to seem weird, but since we've been chatting," she wrings her hands in front of her with a nervous expression on her face. "It's just that your voice sounds oddly familiar."

My cheeks heat at her comment, and I let out an apprehensive laugh.

"Not weird if you listen to podcasts." I shrug as if this happens every day.

It definitely does not.

"Sugar tits! You're from *O positive*, aren't you?" She squeals.

I choke on a laugh, covering my mouth in surprise.

"I've never been called sugar tits before. I like it." My shoulders shake with uncontrollable laughter. Several moments pass before I'm able to catch my breath and confirm her suspicions. We continue to chat for a while before I have to head back and get ready for the entire reason I'm in New York this week.

I've missed you today, Habanero. Where's the party again?

My chest squeezes with a pang of sadness when I see his message.

I've missed you too. Horizon Rooftop Bar, heading to Ka'mani's place on the Upper East side as soon as I get dressed so we have a little extra time together.

Dylan's response comes quickly.

Have a wonderful time, gorgeous. I wish I could be there with you and meet your friends, but I'll see you in the morning.

I reply with a heart emoji, knowing if I continue to message him, I won't finish getting ready in time. Realizing just how late it's gotten, I open the rideshare app to order a ride before shoving my phone in my purse.

Tonight is about my best friend, not about the situationship I've found myself in.

My hair and makeup take over an hour to perfect, but by the time I'm done, I look like I've gotten a full beat done by a makeup artist. A soft smile pulls at my lips when I admire myself in the mirror. I take the couple of steps from the bathroom to where my dress is hanging. After unzipping from the top of the leather corset down to the suit-like material that make up the skirt, I question my life choices when I pull the snug fabric over my hips. I struggle for a few minutes longer than I will ever admit to get the zipper all the way up.

I blow out a frustrated breath and check myself in the mirror. The dress hugs my curves and has my large breasts nearly spilling out while lifting them to the gods.

"Damn, this dress really was a good idea." I admit to the empty room.

I grab my phone from my bag and see my car is nearly here.

"Excuse the fuck out of me, who are you and what did you do with my bestie because she would never wear something so hot out of the house." Ka'Mani twirls her index finger in the air, a request for me to spin for her.

I snort and do as she asks.

"Damn, woman. You look amazing!" She pulls me in for a hug, squeezing me tight.

My heart swells as I take in my favorite person in this world.

"You're one to talk, birthday girl!" I stare with my mouth agape.

She's wearing a pale lavender floor length dress with a slit so high there's no way she has panties on. A ruching effect has the high wasted fabric hiding the small belly she's self-conscious of, not that she has anything to be concerned about. The torso turns into a shear corset until the top turns into a plunging neckline being held together by a thick criss-crossed strap around her neck.

"The fit — especially that color on you, the flawless makeup girl—Carter may have some competition tonight." I fan myself with my hand.

Are you really best friends if you don't threaten to steal each other from each other's relationships?

Ka'Mani laughs and wraps her arms around me again before she pulls me into her apartment. My eyes widen when I take in the spacious living room.

"I knew you were doing well with the company you're with, but dang!" Her style hasn't changed, an ivory leather couch faces a flat screen TV, two sleek matching chairs with black legs and arm rests cage in the coffee table.

We both take a seat on the couch, the cold fabric sending a chill through me.

"Ok, I know you refused to stay with me during your visit since I would have taken off to be with you," she rolls her eyes at my stubbornness, "but since you leave tomorrow, tell me everything I've missed this week."

My mouth forms the biggest smile and I spew out every single detail from the moment I got here until now. Well, not every detail about exactly who Dylan is — just that I met someone. The next hour and a half is spent catching up on both of our lives. We may talk fairly often, but having her in person is so much better.

As soon as I stand to leave when the car is set to arrive Ka'mani insists that we get a picture before leaving. Since she's the birthday girl, obviously I can't deny her. We pose together and take a selfie, she shoots me a mischievous grin and insists on solo pictures.

"Ugh, fine!" I groan in mock outrage.

Roughly forty minutes later, we're walking into the lobby of Horizon and are ushered to the rooftop, where a crowd of people is already waiting for us. Ka'Mani introduces me to everyone as we make our way around the space. I see Carter leaning against the bar and excuse myself to go say hello.

"Our girl looks hot tonight." I elbow him in the ribs, gently taunting him, and he snorts.

"She always looks good." He shrugs. "It's good seeing you. Have a good night, kid."

Carter turns around and walks into the crowd. I arch a brow, confused. Before I can think more of it, a loud scream comes from Ka'Mani, and I rush to her side where I find her holding an obnoxiously large bouquet of pink, purple and orange flowers.

"What's wrong?" I ask, out of breath.

"Dylan fucking Bryant!" She squeals, her eyes wide and locked on me, "Are you kidding me?"

I glance down at the card, and my cheeks flush when I read the note.

She then shoves her phone in my face. The display shows a post of the pictures she took of us at her place before we left on her social media feed with a comment.

@DylanBryantOfficial: Holy hell, my girl looks good. Can't wait to meet you, Ka'Mani! Have a good night!

"Ma'am, you need to share with the class, because you left a few chapters out." She drags me over to a table where several of her closest friends follow to eavesdrop and join in on the conversation.

"So, what had happened was..."

My suitcase is packed and sitting next to the bench I'm waiting at just after sunrise. A cool breeze rushes over me, and I pull Dylan's jacket tight around my body, knowing I'm going to return it today. My gaze lifts to find him approaching with a familiar white paper bag and two large hot takeout cups. I grin at him and shake my head.

"You were the talk of the party last night, sir." I call out to him as he approaches.

He sits down next to me with a shy smile tugging at his lips.

"Did she like the flowers?" He asks and hands me my cup.

My responding nod makes his smile widen. He leans in and presses his soft lips to mine; our mouths and tongues work together, deepening the kiss into something extraordinarily hot. My heart races when his free hand wraps around the back of my neck, holding me in place.

We part after several delicious moments, and my eyes lock on his.

"And the tickets." I wrap my arm around his middle, burying my head in the crook his neck. "You really didn't need to do all of that."

"Habanero, she's your best friend." He pulls me closer to him, "if we're going to make a real go of this, even if it's long distance, I am going to do my damnedest to show you and everyone you love how much you mean to me, which includes them by extension."

I pull back to look at his face, my mind whirling over how serious his tone is.

"The question is, are you really in for a long-distance relationship, for now?"

Chapter Fourteen

Five weeks later

"One of my favorite things about hosting this podcast is being able to share others' sexcapades with the world that they never would have tried if they hadn't found their first "O" with a smutty book or two." I say into the microphone, my lips are in a wide smile as I look at my friend sitting next to me. "I have one of my best friends, Fallon, with me today who is going to share some of her positive experiences."

A silent notification window pops up on my computer screen, letting me know another person has joined the recording session. I grin even wider because I know Fallon is going to lose her mind.

"We know everything about one another," I chuckle into the micro-phone, "but can you tell my listeners a little about yourself?"

She smiles while she twists her fingers in her lap and leans forward to speak.

"Hi y'all! I'm Fallon. Talking about myself is weird—does anyone really like to do that?" She begins to ramble. "I'm married to a ridiculously sexy farmer."

"I'll second that." I interject, and we both erupt into a fit of giggles.

"My passion besides reading is animal rescue. Ryker and I are actually working on renovating an old barn on our property into a space for a shelter so we can start our own rescue."

Her golden retriever, Marlow, sits up from where he's lying on the floor next to her and lays his head in her lap as she continues to speak.

"We have two dogs that are actually here with Mads and I today and a fox that stayed at home." She pauses to think about what to say next. "Don't take that as I'm encouraging anyone to just go out and bring a fox into your home. Mr. Feeny has been living on my husband's property for years and still lives outside. They've just become fond of one another and the little guy has made himself at home and part of our family."

When she is more comfortable, we get into the topic of her favorite author, K. D. Smalls, and she absolutely lights up when the subject shifts into why choose books.

"Oh my god! Mads," she squeals into the mic. "The first time I read a multiple partner scene, it was in this book, and holy shit!"

Fallon waves her hand in front of her face, fanning herself dramatical-ly.

"You know my husband; he's possessive as hell, so there is no way he would let another person into our bed to try anything like that, but – we got a few dildos and worked our way up to including them into our sexy time – Oh. My. God! Ten out of ten!"

A soft chuckle vibrates through the headphones.

"I didn't expect you to go that hard before I could introduce you to K.D. Smalls." I snort and signal my silent guest to speak.

"Hey girl! I've heard so much about you." K.D.'s voice is warm, as if she didn't just hear about someone kind of recreating a scene she wrote.

Fallon's cheeks are as red as a tomato when the voice of her favorite author comes through the headphones.

"I hate you." She throws a plush dog toy at me, which squeaks loudly causing the three of us to laugh.

"Don't hate her! I love that you enjoyed that scene. It was a blast to write." K. D.'s reassurance seems to bring Fallon out of embarrassment. "I love, love, love that my characters inspired you to try something new with your partner. That scene was so spicy too, I don't blame you!"

"It's true, K.D. knows how to write good spice." I chime in again.

"I really hope my stories and characters can empower more readers to experience new things in safe ways. There is so much more to come too!"

Time seems to speed by, our conversation with K.D. continues well after recording ends. After she signs off, Fallon and I move over to my couch with her dogs, and we chat a while longer. She shifts the topic to my love life, and my cheeks flush under her scrutinizing gaze.

Memories of the past five weeks flood my mind. Dylan and I have made it a point to video chat once a day if not more. Since flying isn't something I'm comfortable with, he's made a priority to get to me on his one day off a week, three of the past five, all without pressuring me to get on a plane. If anything, that fact alone has made my feelings for him even stronger, and in such a short amount of time, which is baffling.

Fallon swoons over Dylan's actions when I share everything and tells me to bring him over the next time he comes out. She leaves not long after, having to get back to her place since she and Ryker have a date night planned. After I say goodbye, I return to my computer to get the content for the episode uploaded to my editor's shared drive. The moment it completes, I hear a notification from the same social media platform Dylan first contacted me through.

I click on the open tab on my desktop and see a message from @BetweenTheLines. My brow arches when I see the preview of the content.

@BetweenTheLines:

Hey Girlie…

My heart drops to my stomach when I see those two words that every girl dreads.

There are several ways I can handle this. One, ignore it and let myself silently spiral. Two, read it and, depending on what I find, cut Dylan off without a word. Or three, see what he has to say before I open the message.

A few years ago, number three never would have been an option. Now, I fear it's the only one I can cope with, no matter what the truth is. My heart beats violently in my chest while I hype myself up enough to make the call. When I finally grab my phone from my desk, I find Dylan's contact and press the button for a video call.

Five seconds go by before my call is declined.

The searing pain of unshed tears wells in the corners of my eyes. I blow out a breath and lower the device to my lap. My breath comes out in shallow pants as my mind begins to rush down the rabbit hole of "what if's."

The rational part of my brain tries to remind me that there is a time difference and he may be in rehearsal. It's not like he answers every time

I call him. So, to keep myself from drowning in a mix of Ben and Jerry's and a bottle of cheap wine, I dive into housework.

Knowing I stay on top of everything as much as possible, there isn't much to do, so I decide to try my hand at interior design. How hard could it be to move furniture around myself?

Roughly five hours later, sweat drips from my temples as I push my couch into yet another position. I've re-arranged each room multiple times - only to end up with everything in its original spot in the end.

My ears perk up when I hear a loud knock against my front door. I cautiously cross the space and peek out the peephole. Something pink is distorting the view, so I pull open the door expecting to see Elle wrapped in her pink robe only; that's not who I find at all.

"Hey, Habanero." Dylan's sinfully talented lips turn up into a wicked grin. A ridiculously oversized bouquet of pink roses are in his arms.

"Oh, my God! What are you doing here?" I shriek out with excitement, my earlier concern completely forgotten.

I'm still trying to catch my breath from the last orgasm when Dylan saunters into my bathroom. I roll my eyes as he disappears. He's really proud of himself tonight for getting a first of mine. The evidence is still dripping down my legs and all over my sheet, and my cheeks heat at the memory of how it felt to squirt for him, especially when he talks me through an orgasm. *Jesus.*

My bubble of serotonin comes crashing to a halt when my phone dings from the bedside table. I grab the device and see the forgotten message along with another one from @BetweenTheLines. My gaze drifts to see Dylan is still out of sight. I let out a deep breath, tap to open.

@BetweenTheLines:

Hey Girlie – can we chat?

Listen, I don't know how to start this, and I know you don't owe me anything. I've always declared myself a girls' girl, and while I realize that in some of the posts and allowing some of the comments from people have made me not appear so, I can't sit on the sidelines and let you get hurt because of a man. I haven't posted anything because I didn't want you to be blindsided, but I've been getting a lot of tips that Dylan and Marie are getting close. Like physically and romantically close. Whether they're real or not, I don't know - but I wanted you to have the information to do with as you wish.

My emotions are written clear as day on my face because when Dylan re-emerges he's at my side in an instant.

"What's going on with Marie?" I ask, my voice is soft as I try not to let the tremble of anger show in my words.

Chapter Fifteen

Four weeks ago

My mouth pops open with a big yawn as I step into my dressing room. A ride directly from the airport to the theatre made the most sense so I could get an extra couple of hours of sleep. I've never been so happy to collapse on my puke-green couch than I am at this moment. Before I allow myself to doze off I pull my phone from my jacket pocket and send a message to Mads letting her know I'm back safe.

Her response is instantaneous.

I miss you too, Dyl. I'm still in shock that you came out for just a day. Get some rest, call me when you can.

My lips pull up into a soft smile as I doze off.

I startle awake some time later to see Marie kneeling next to me, her hands resting on the waistband of my pants.

Present

Mads' eyes are filled with a mix of anger and hurt. Her body goes rigid when my hands rest on her thighs.

"What's going on with Marie?" She's trying to be strong but the pain is clear in how soft she asks the question.

I blow out a heavy breath.

"That's actually, at least partially why I came back out without warning." I chew on the inside of my cheek knowing this could all be over by the time I'm done talking. "I took a week off so I could stay with you — if that's alright. But if you don't want me to, I understand."

Mads glares at me, crossing her arms against her chest trying to hide from me.

"The first time I came out here, do you remember I went straight back to the theatre instead of going home?"

She nods silently waiting for the bomb to drop.

"I fell asleep as soon as I sent you a text. Honestly, I barely remember seeing your response before passing out." I climb to my feet and begin to pace the length of her room.

"Dyl," her voice is softer and much kinder than I probably deserve. "What happened?"

"When I woke up, Marie was there. She tried–" I swallow hard. "Well, she had gotten my jeans unbuttoned by the time I came to."

Mads eyes go wide, her anger is more prominent now.

"I made her stop, I promise you – you are the only one I want." The words come out in a rush, emotion and dread get stuck in my throat causing me to choke out the rest of my thoughts. "I haven't gone in early since, when I've flown home from here if it doesn't make sense to go back to my place I've been getting a room at the building you stayed at for the day since it's so close to the theatre. I've been avoiding being anywhere near her as much as I can."

Mads soft fingers wrap around my hands, forcing me to stop moving. I glance down at her to see tears streaking down her cheeks.

"Marie assaulted you, Dyl." Mads says gently. "I'm not upset with you. Not in the least."

A weight lifts from me, and I fall to my knees as tears begin to rush from my own eyes.

She wraps her arms around my shoulders, holding me tight while I relay everything from the past month. Any time I've been within arm's reach, Marie tries to get grabby, and even though she's been informed – not only by me – that I'm with Mads, she still tries. Her behavior has become so foul that I'm ready to negotiate an early termination of my contract. Part of my motive for coming here this week is to make that decision. I may come across as a simp for this admission but – my mind relaxes around my girl and this decision is too big to make on my own.

Our hands are tangled together while we stroll through the town I've been to several times, yet we've never had the time to leave her apartment. When we walk into a quaint coffee shop, I recognize the name, The Caffeinated Pumpkin. Mads has mentioned this place before. My senses are overwhelmed with so many variations of pumpkin, I stumble backwards. I allow my eyes to roam over the glass cases that hold a variety of pastries. It's when my gaze lands on a cinnamon swirl pumpkin croissant filled with cream cheese icing that a shrill noise echoes through the little shop.

"He's here? You brought him here!" An energetic woman rushes around the counter and comes to a quick halt before she can get to me. "Oh my God, I know, I knew, but seeing him here is shocking."

My body is still as stone while I wait to see what Mads' reaction is before I decide what to do.

"Elle, this is Dylan. Dylan, this is Elle." She shakes her head, chuckling. "She's my landlord and one of my best friends."

I chuckle and extend my hand in greeting. Elle's cheeks flush as she accepts my offering.

"Sorry. I've been a musical nerd since I was a kid." She rambles, "I used to drive Ryker crazy by making him watch any musical I could get my hands on."

My lips turn up into a genuine smile.

"It's a pleasure to meet you. No judgment here." I chuckle, "I reacted similarly when I first met Venus Van Trager during their first run on Broadway."

Elle's eyes go wide as her hand squeezes mine even tighter before she realizes what she's doing and eventually releases me.

"Shut the front door! You've met Venus Van Trager?" She squeals.

The rest of the week is much more relaxed, so few people know who I am. Sure they know the show I'm in, but since I'm not from the original cast on the soundtrack that was released, my name isn't the household name like theirs are. It's a bit freeing in a sense. After my confession to Mads, I expected to be thrown out. Sure, people know that assault against men happens, but no one talks about it. I was half afraid she wouldn't believe me. I shake the worries from my mind knowing it's no longer necessary.

Frustration has been brewing in me knowing I am headed back tomorrow. I step into Mads office to find her comparing a physical day planner with an online calendar. She's so invested in what she's doing she doesn't notice my presence until I lean down and press a soft kiss against the column of her neck.

"Hey! I thought you were sleeping." She drops what she's doing and spins to face me, a gorgeous smile on her lips.

Dropping to my knees in front of her, I wrap my arms around her waist and stare up at her.

"I love this place; everyone you've introduced me to has been incredible. The town itself is fantastic, and is exactly the type of place I'd like to retire to." My heart beats so harshly, I'm surprised she can't hear it. "You know, I wish I could stay here. But being on the stage is my dream."

"I know that." Mads voice is soft and encouraging when she speaks. "Dyl, we'll figure it out."

After blowing out a steadying breath, I ask the craziest question I ever will.

"We may not have known each other or have been together very long." I pause, raising my gaze to hers. My need for her to see how sincere I am is so strong. "Come home with me."

"Come home with me."

Dylan's words echo through my mind while my eyes remain fixed on his. Nothing in his expression or tone tells me he's joking, but there is no way he could possibly be asking me to move to New York with him.

"You mean like," my pitch increases with my confusion. "Stay at your place for like a week?"

His arms are still wrapped around me as he helps me stand and guides me out to my couch. I allow myself to get lost in the feel of his strong, muscular form enveloping me.

"No, my sweet Habanero." A gentle laugh bubbles up from his chest. "Move in with me."

"What?" I gasp. "That's a huge step."

So many scenarios run through my mind. Yes, moving there could be amazing, and I did love being in a place that is so full of life. But there are so many what if's, we haven't known each other that long.

"Are you sure?" I ask as I struggle to calm my thoughts.

Dylan's face breaks into a smile. The way his face lights up is like a balm that is healing parts of me I didn't know were still in shambles.

"Yes, I'm sure." He lifts my chin so I can't look away. "I can't imagine a future without you by my side. Life is too short not to go for what you want, and Maddox, you are what I want."

Chapter Sixteen

We've spent the last day talking about the pros and cons of what it could mean for Mads to join me in New York. Even if I'm entirely in this relationship, no matter what her decision is, I hate having to leave without it. After snapping a picture of the plane pulling into the terminal and sending it off to Mads, I slide the device back into my pocket. It's been nice not using it for anything other than taking pictures of her and us this week. My life is so ingrained in social media that when I'm performing, I have to post as often as possible to keep people interested. I'm not quite ready to be *on,* one hundred percent of the time.

Several minutes later when my group is called to board, I pull my Giants cap down so the rim partially hides my face. I drag my backpack onto my shoulder and cross the waiting area to have my boarding pass scanned. The flight is early enough in the morning that not too many people are here, so I'm happy to see I have a row to myself.

We're in the air when I lose whatever hope for patience I have left. I find it impossible to avoid my phone any longer. Not because I want to rejoin the land of social media, but because I hate not knowing which way Maddox is leaning. After I pull it back out, I see she's replied with a heart emoji and a message that twists my insides.

Mads:

I miss you already. No matter what I decide, I will come out next weekend for the week.

Asking her to pick up her life especially so close to the holidays is a one in a million chance, but even so I would be kicking myself every day if I threw away my shot at having her with me full time. A deep groan rumbles up from my chest. Never in my wildest dreams did I have falling for a woman who lives halfway across the country on my bingo card for this year. I toss my head back against the headrest of my seat and close my eyes. Thoughts of what if's and what could be dance through my mind with every passing second.

Some time later I startle awake, and my eyes fly open as the plane comes to a stop.

When the hell did I fall asleep and how the fuck did I remain unconscious during landing?

A crackle sounds overhead as the pilot's voice takes over the cabin.

"Thank you for joining us on JetAir today. The current local time here at JFK International Airport is ten twenty-two AM. We hope to have you fly with us again soon."

We're given the all-clear to deplane ten minutes later. I grab my carry-on and walk as quickly as my feet will carry me toward the baggage claim. There is no time to rest now that I'm back home. Once my suitcase is back in my possession, I glance up to see Annie standing by the door with a knowing glint in her eyes. A chuckle escapes me when she waggles her eyebrows at me. She pulls me in for a hug when I approach.

"Welcome home. How's our girl?" Annie pulls away, turning toward the door, and I follow dutifully.

"She's perfect as always." I smirk before dragging my hand down my face. "Thanks for the ride. How was it this week?"

I'm able to make out Annie shrugging from my periphery; she's hesitant while she tries to form the words. My gaze tracks every subtle change of her features while she decides how much to share.

"Whatever happened with Marie that made you leave — no one blames you for — but she's been on the warpath since you left." A shiver vibrates through my friend's body. "You know how she acts like she owns all of us? Her attitude toward everyone was even worse this week."

The bright morning sun shines through the window of my third-floor bedroom. The blinds do little to keep the beginning of the day at bay. My eyes flutter open under the assault of the obnoxiously bright giant star. I let out a groan when I sit up, not ready to face the day. My lips pull into a smile as the scent of apple cider donut coffee fills my lungs. The sudden addiction to all things apple cider is obviously credited to my delectably spicy woman. I force myself to stand, and grab my phone from my nightstand before dragging my feet toward the kitchen where my freshly brewed caffeine is waiting for me. My favorite mug is set next to the pot where I left it last night when I scheduled the time to brew. I pull up Mads' contact and tap the icon to video chat while I pour the steaming liquid into my mug. The call is declined as I lift the drink to my lips.

I arch my brow and glance at the time; she's usually awake by now. My phone begins to ring with an incoming call, I see Mads name. Swiping the screen to answer before I lift the device to my ear.

"Good morning, Gorgeous." My voice is still rough with sleep.

There's a nervous edge to her voice as she responds.

"Hey, Dyl," there is a softness in her tone that makes my heart stutter in my chest. "I've made a decision."

The illusion of time comes to a sudden stop when I hear her words. I suck in a sharp breath and lower the mug to the counter while I wait for her to tell me one way or another. My fingers grip the edge of the counter, anxious to know what's next.

"Tell me." I breathe.

There's a pause and then a soft knock on my front door.

"Mads?" I ask while I move toward whoever thinks seven in the morning is an appropriate time to come over.

"So-"

I reach out, wrapping my fingers around the metal knob and twist before pulling the door open to see a raven-haired firecracker with a sinful smile spread across her soft features.

Chapter Seventeen

The night before

Anxiety churns in my stomach when I pull out of the drop-off lane at Hollow Heights airport. The taste of him lingers on my tongue. I groan and set out toward the place I call home. It is my home. This apartment may have only been mine for a year and a half, but I've called this town home my entire life. My mind spins when I finally park outside of The Caffeinated Pumpkin.

Elle is standing behind the display case when I walk in, a welcoming smile on her lips that falters as soon as she gets a good look at me.

"Bestie Boo!" Elle shouts with an anxious note in her voice; behind her I see Fallon rush out her hand resting on her protruding pregnant belly.

They're both at my side within a moment.

"I don't know why I'm such a mess." The words come out in a choked sob.

Elle wraps an arm around my shoulders.

"Where's Dylan?" Fallon's question makes my lips pull into a sad smile.

My shoulders tense when I catch my breath enough to answer.

"He had to go home. But-" I swallow thickly and drop my face into my hands. "I'm being ridiculous, I know that."

The two of them cage me in a hug holding me tight for several moments before releasing me.

"Do you want to talk here or back at home?" Elle offers.

Putting on a brave face, I shake my head.

"He asked me to move to New York." I blow out a breath.

Fallon and Elle look at each other before turning their questioning gazes on me.

"Uh, babe." Fallon speaks up this time. "Why the hell are you still here?"

Elle nods silently in agreement.

"This is my home!" After a beat of silence, I glance down and stare at my hands in my lap. "Can I really just leave the only place I've really known?"

Fallon's shoulders shake with laughter.

"Love, you've read my story, right?" She snorts out and continues, "I left the only place I knew after everything went to shit. At least you'd be leaving here with only positive memories. Who's to say you can't come back?"

I sit up straight, my eyes drift back and forth between the two as my friend's words set in.

"I need to book a flight." My phone is in my hand before I finish my thought. "Wait, how do I book a flight?"

My friends start giggling, Fallon snags my phone from my hands. Elle pulls me to my feet and shouts over her shoulder to the other person working that she's leaving early.

"I'll help you pack, Fallon will get your travel figured out." Elle's amusement is clear with every word spoken.

They completely take over, we all pile into Elle's car and head back to my place. We step inside, my mind is set on digging through my closet for a suitcase. A small cool hand on my forearm pulls me from my thoughts. "What are your must haves for the first few weeks until I can get your stuff shipped?"

I begin to panic and pace the length of my apartment, Fallon glances up from my phone as she places it on the kitchen table.

"You're set to leave on a red eye tonight so we have time."

Elle claps her hands with excitement.

"Alright make a list, I assume you need your computer and podcast stuff. We can wrap all of the fragile items in your clothes to keep them safe."

The packing for my flight is less stressful than I expected. When that part is done and I have to leave instructions for Elle to pack up the rest of my life, I worry I'm asking too much of her.

"You're sure?" I chew the inside of my cheek while I wait for her response.

"Woman, be selfish for once." She rolls her eyes at me.

I rush around town to say my goodbyes to the few people I'm sad to leave over the rest of the afternoon.

My two friends get me to the airport an hour before departure, my stomach is in knots as I say goodbye.

"I'm getting on a plane for this man." I sob when we're standing on the sidewalk of the drop-off lane I was in just this morning. Both of their arms are wrapped tightly around me, Fallon's shoulders shake. Taking a step back, my mouth drops open when I realize she's laughing.

"Sorry, babe." She wipes tears from the corners of her eyes. "That's how we know you're in love with him. You didn't even leave the state for college because the thought of flying farther terrifies you. And now you're going halfway across the country for your man."

Dylan's FaceTime request comes through as I step out of the cab. I hit decline knowing he'll recognize my surroundings, and I've had my heart set on a romantic gesture that would make a Hallmark exec swoon. As soon as I get my bags upstairs onto his floor, I press the icon to call him back.

"Good morning, gorgeous." His voice is rough with sleep.

I try my best to keep my excitement at bay.

"Hey, Dyl," I say in greeting, trying to keep my voice low, unsure if he can hear me through the walls. "I've made a decision."

I quickly close the distance between the landing and his door.

"Tell me." His voice is barely a whisper.

I mute my end of the phone and knock on his door; my lips pull up into a wide smile.

"Mads?" he calls for me again.

I click the mute button off so he can hear me again

"So-"

The door opens quickly, like he's ready to slap whoever dared show up so early.

My smile turns sinful when I see his glorious muscular chest is on full display.

"My heart is with you; my home is wherever you are." I step forward, resting my hand against his chest. I can feel the steady thrum of the organ pumping under my fingers. "Besides, I can bring my dreams with me." I chuckle and nod toward my suitcases.

Chapter Eighteen

My feet carry me forward, and I lift Mads into my arms. An infectious giggle erupts from her when I spin and carry her into my apartment. My mouth finds hers when I lay her down on my couch. She whimpers when my tongue delves past her parted lips. Her body responds so beautifully when my hands roam the curves and valleys of her delicious body. A hitch of her breath when I dip my hand under the hem of her T-shirt sends a jolt of need to my dick.

"Fuck," I groan as I feel her grind against my length.

Mads giggles, her hands reaching for my neck to pull me back down to continue the passionate exchange.

"Wait," I sit up quickly, startling us both. "How did you get here?"

Her cheeks are already flushed from our kiss yet seem to brighten even more.

"I-I," she stumbles over the words. "Fallon got me a flight late last night. She and Elle helped me pack the necessities, and they'll send the rest next week."

That's when I notice the two large suitcases still sitting in the hallway outside of my open door. I glance over at her, a renewed excitement at the realization, and lean in pressing my lips against hers once more.

"Stay here." I quickly get the luggage inside and close the door behind me before sauntering back toward her.

By the time I return to her, Mads is sitting with her back against the couch like she's always been here. As if she's always been meant to be here, to be with me.

I drop to my knees, between her legs. She reaches out, dragging her fingers through my unkempt hair. My lips turn up in a wicked grin as I hook my fingers under the waistband of her dark leggings, dragging them over her hips and down her thighs. I smirk when I find she's bare underneath.

She lets out a needy breath when I toss them to the side. I grip her thighs and pull her to the edge of the couch and shove her legs apart. My gaze remain on her dark eyes when I dip my head and press my lips against the creamy flesh of her thick thighs, trailing kisses to her wet slit. I suck in a deep breath, taking in the unique scent that is entirely her. Without another thought, I lean in, my tongue darting out to lick up the proof of her arousal.

"Dylan!" She calls out my name like a prayer. "Please, make me come!"

A dark chuckle passes my lips as I slowly repeat the motion. Enjoying every moment of torture I cause when I lightly flick my tongue against her clit, not giving in to her demands. She holds out longer than I expect before both hands delve into my hair and she grabs hold. Using the unruly mess as handle bars while she takes control of her own pleasure and grinds her glistening pussy against my face. I sense when she's about to fall over the edge, the movements become erratic, her words for me become even more filthy.

"You like when I use your pretty face as my own personal fuck toy, don't you?" She pants out.

I groan appreciatively in response as I slide a finger inside her pussy, curling it to find the sweet spot inside her.

"Oh, fuck yes, Dylan!" She cries out as her hips buck up, pressing the tiny bundle of nerves harder against my tongue, looking for a little more pressure. Her walls convulse around my finger when she finds her release. Sobs of pleasure wrack through her until she comes down from the high.

She breathes out a satisfied sigh, a low chuckle rumbles up my chest. I climb to my feet, pulling Mads with me.

"I need you in bed right now."

Mads lets out a surprised squeal, laughter bubbles out from her when I toss her over my shoulder. She smacks my ass while hanging upside down, her giddiness fills me with my own excitement.

I lower her to the floor, her hands are on my shorts as soon as she's free from my hold. We make quick work of what little clothing we have on. She bats her eyes at me, silently pleading with me.

"Baby, not yet." I groan when she climbs on the bed, the beautifully full hips and round plump ass, sways as she crawls away from me. "I need to feel that pussy choking my cock."

We've only come up for air from one another mere moments ago yet, seeing Mads drag one of my *Her Final Shot* T-shirts over her head has my dick is already coming back to life.

"Fuck, you look good, gorgeous." I shake my head;

Her face brightens when she sees the way I'm watching her. She pulls her hair up into a messy bun before she climbs back into bed and buries her face in my chest. I wrap my arms around her, securing her as close to my heart as I can.

A thought comes to mind. I grip her chin, tilting her face to raise so her gaze is on me.

"How would you feel about publicly and officially announcing our relationship?"

Her expression freezes, and I sit up, confused.

"What?"

"I just, I don't know. I thought I was moving across the country for a fling." She deadpans and shrugs nonchalantly before she unravels in a fit of laughter. "I'm happy to go official publicly; but, how?"

I fight back my own smile.

"Smartass, come here." I pull her in for a kiss and snap a picture with my phone. When we separate, her eyes remain closed for several minutes while I pull up a social media profile for someone I never expected to contact. I attach the picture and type a short message.

@DylanBryantOfficial:

> You can be the one to share our hard launch. She's officially a New Yorker and I'm not giving her up.

Their response is swift.

@BetweenTheLines:

> Holy shit! Wow, thanks for the exclusive!

"I hate you." Mads groans and flops back onto the mattress.

"No, you don't." I snort, continuing to type on my phone. Her device chimes as soon as I put mine down, and a proud smile spreads across my face.

Mads crawls across me to check her notifications; her cheeks flush the most beautiful pink when she sees what I shared. Every picture I've taken of us over the past month is now out there with a declaration I hadn't yet verbalized with her, yet.

@DylanBryantOfficial: Nothing could be better than being able to come home to the love of my life every night. Our future is as bright as you, Habanero. I love you, gorgeous.

@DylanBryantOfficial Nothing could be better than being able to come home to the love of my life every night. Our future is as bright as you, Habanero. I love you, gorgeous.

Chapter Nineteen

My body is sore from just how much fucking we did last night once Dylan got home. I roll onto my side and reach out for him. The sheets are cold.

Ugh, he keeps doing this to me.

Reluctantly, I force myself out of bed. According to my phone, it's only four in the morning.

"What the hell." I whisper into the empty room.

I climb out of bed, grabbing one of Dylan's hoodies hanging on the closet door. I pull it over my head, and walk out in search of him. The apartment has an open floor plan, it's easy to see most of the place. Twinkling lights from the small Christmas tree in the corner nearly distracts from the light coming from underneath the spare room's door. A yawn escapes me as I cross the space. I notice the door isn't latched shut before I reach the door. My mouth pops open when I press the door open to see Dylan rummaging through the room. Boxes upon boxes filled with odds and ends.

"What?" Is the only thing that I can say standing in the doorway watching him.

Dylan jumps up, startled at my arrival. His eyes light up with excitement when he sees me.

"I didn't wake you, did I?"

Still at a loss for words, shaking my head is all I'm able to do in response.

"You need a designated space for you. I've been using this room primarily for storage." He shrugs as if what he's offering is no big deal. "You moved your entire life for me; the least I can do is give you a podcast studio and office."

Dylan saunters toward me with a tender expression in his eyes. He closes the distance between the two of us in just a few steps. His mouth crashes against mine. My lips part in a gasp, and I moan into his mouth at the welcome distraction.

"I started looking into soundproofing on the way to work last night too," Dylan says smoothly when he straightens.

My shoulders shake with silent laughter.

"You don't need to do that; I have things to combat noise." I shake my head again, unable to fight the smile tugging on my lips. "I love you, Dyl."

Dylan's arms wrap tightly around my waist, his bright gaze full of adoration.

"I love you too, Habanero." He presses a soft kiss to my forehead before releasing me. "Let's go back to bed, gorgeous."

He waggles his brows suggestively at me when I don't move right away.

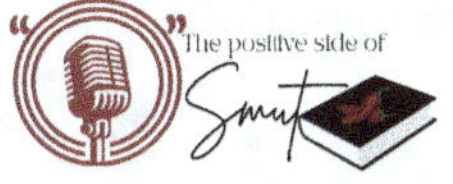

A week later

One of my favorite narrator's, Lauren Beck, sultry voice, sounds through my earbuds as she portrays an anxious librarian named Hope getting railed by a shadow daddy.

It's way hotter than should be legal. Don't judge me.

Simultaneously, the album featuring the original cast of Her Final Shot plays through Dylan's Bluetooth speakers while I finish connecting my computer. I suck in a sharp breath when the clip for connecting my podcast microphone to my desk pinches my finger.

"Fuck," I hiss, my lips flattening into a tight line while I scold myself.

It's not like I've never put this together before.

My movements are much more calculated as I continue perfecting my setup. After a couple of hours, the task is finished, and I let out a sigh of relief.

When I check my phone, I realize I only have a little bit of time before Dylan will be home. His usual routine on no-performance days starts at the gym and then spends at least a good portion of the day with some of the show's company. Today, he's invited everyone here, a way to welcome me to the city.

Rushing to the bathroom, I turn on the shower and undress quickly. My lips part with a pained squeal when the cold water touches my skin.

Ignoring the shock, I go through the motions of washing my hair. After I lather, rinse, and repeat the process with my conditioner, I move on to my body. A violent shiver runs through my body when the water finally warms. Just in time for me to be finished.

Of course.

I quickly dry off and move back into the bedroom. My lips pull into a delighted smile when I easily find the dark gray graphic T-shirt I've been hoping to wear. The words Feral Girl Fall are set above an adorable trash panda with a scarf wrapped around its cute little neck while the furry paws rest on two small pumpkins, pinecones, and leaves cage the precious guy in.

Do I have it in every color for every season? Yes.

Do I have the business' website bookmarked? Also, yes.

When you like something, you buy it in every color. It's a girl thing, right?

Right?

I pop my earbud back in and walk back into the living room. A chuckle bubbles from my lips when I hear Lauren's voice go on about hybrid shadow daddy babies. Why is this so good? My gaze drifts up when I sit on the couch, and a scream that would make Jamie Lee Curtis proud escapes. Marie is standing inside our front door.

"Holy shit," I clutch my chest trying to relearn how to breathe. "Sorry, you scared me. I wasn't expecting anyone yet."

I glance around, slightly confused as to how she got inside.

"Where's Dylan?"

Marie scoffs.

"Why are you here?"

I open my mouth to speak and close it, unsure of what to say.

"Ok, um." I force out, a need to play hostess kicks in. "Would you like anything to drink?"

My heart stops for a second when she crosses her arms against her chest. She's wearing a colorless long sleeve shirt that looks like it hasn't been washed in a while and a pair of dark leggings. There is a taser visible in her hand. I pause, taking a step back.

"Why are *you* here?" She repeats.

"I-I live here." My response comes out in a stutter.

Marie advances toward me with a look of pure terror.

"You think you can take him from me?" She snarls, "This is my show! He's supposed to be with me!"

The crackle of the taser has my body going rigid and then everything blacks out.

Chapter Twenty

My feet move swiftly as I race up the stairs, my hair and body are drenched with sweat. A buddy from the gym baited me into a conversation about the Giants which turned into a debate about Archie Manning.

The fucker.

I still have twenty minutes before anyone should be showing up, that's plenty of time to shower. Well unless Mads wants to join me. Maybe I should leave a sock on my door knob just in case. Chuckling at myself when I approach the door in question, I freeze when I hear a loud crackle of electricity from inside my apartment.

I reach out for the knob and swallow thickly as I twist it, cautiously letting myself inside.

My eyes go wide when I see Marie holding Mads in a choked hold with a neon blue taser pressed against her jugular.

"What in the actual fuck." It comes out just barely a whisper, no one else can hear.

Tears stream silently down Mads' cheeks, leaving dark streaks of makeup in their wake. Her warm brown eyes are pleading from where she stands frozen in place.

I suck in a breath and direct my attention to Marie.

"What's going on?" My voice is steadier than I feel.

Marie squeezes Mads tighter, I raise my hands showing I'm not going to fight. Thankfully she loosens her hold, and Mads gasps for air. Every fiber of my being wants to throw Marie out of my window, head-first - but that will land me in jail.

"You are mine! The day you signed the contract you were mine!" She shouts in a choked sob. "Why does she get what's mine?"

Excuse the fuck out of me.

"If you let her go we can talk about that, but if you hurt her, we won't be able to be together." The words taste bitter on my tongue.

Marie's eyes soften momentarily but change to a vile expression just as quickly.

A shadowy figure appears beside me, and I glance over to see a police officer with a gun aimed at Marie, and Mads by default.

If anything happens to her a window will be the least of Marie's problems.

There is an exchange that I barely hear between the police officers that have somehow ended up in my apartment and the monster holding my girl against her will. I concentrate on Mads never allowing my gaze to leave hers, trying to reassure her somehow.

My body is humming with adrenaline as I try to find a way in to get to Mads. Time seems to stand still and move at the blink of an eye at the same time. Every scenario I play out in my head ends terribly no matter how I spin it.

Anger radiates through me and I take a step forward ready to do what I'm not sure. But staying still is no longer an option.

An officer steps in front of me before I'm able to get any closer, obscuring my vision. I hear a thud and a scream simultaneously and I shove the policeman out of the way to find Marie unconscious on the floor and Mads collapsed next to her, her hands clawing at her neck.

My feet move before my brain and I rush to her side, I pull Mads into my arms, her entire body shaking after the ordeal.

"Mads, I'm here. I'm here." I repeat gently into her hair. "Habanero, I've got you, baby."

Her arms wrap tightly around my neck as I pull her to her feet. I carefully guide her to the couch and set her down. My attention turns back to the group of police officers in my apartment.

"What the fuck is going on. Who called you?" I choke, pulling Mads into my chest when I lower myself to join her. "Don't get me wrong, I'm glad, but what the fuck."

I allow my eyes to travel around the apartment.

"Seriously, where did y'all come from?"

A tall, dark skin gentleman steps forward and kneels in front of us. He has a warmth about him that makes me feel an instant comfort.

"We received a call from your neighbor. They heard a scream after noticing someone they didn't recognize enter your apartment."

The explanation goes on for a while before they begin to question Mads and me. My anger from the ordeal only intensifies when they try to separate us.

"If you think for one god damn second I'm going to let her out of my sight after what she just went through," I growl.

The officer who seems to be in charge shakes his head at the *interrogation specialist* which seems to get him to switch gears.

Marie is taken out in cuffs when she regains consciousness shouting some nonsense about her contract and mine.

Annie and Cassie arrive a moment later. Shit, I completely forgot about the get together. The two girls rush over to Mads, ignoring me entirely.

The officer in charge jerks his head for me to join him when he sees we have company. I reluctantly release her after placing a soft kiss on her temple and promising to return in a minute.

"We're nearly done, from what Marie has shared so far, she was under the impression that your contract with the show was supposed to include that you'd um-" he glances around awkwardly, "-date her. Exclusively."

My mouth pops open at the revelation.

"Uh, I'm all for sex workers having the right to do as they please it's their body after all but um — I'm a one-woman, man and she's my one." I point to Mads. "But, that's not legal, is it?"

The officer snorts at my question.

"No, not at all."

"I have a copy of my contract in my safe," I point toward Mads' office, where I keep all the legal documents. "My agent and I reviewed it before signing. There was no mention of Marie anywhere in it."

He shrugs as if he's not worried about it.

Ok.

Annie and Cassie help Mads into our room to clean herself up while the rest of the officers leave. I lean against the door when it's finally closed and let out a shaky breath. Giving myself only a moment to regain my composure I walk into my room to see the three women wrapped in an embrace.

"I know I shouldn't be jealous-" my throat tightens, "-but I need my girl alone right now."

Annie is the first one to step back, she snags a pillow from the bed and throws it at me. We smile weakly at each other, Cassie steps back and wraps an arm around Annie's waist.

"Hey, Habanero." I whisper to Mads who flings herself onto me. "We're ok?"

I'm not sure why the last part comes out as a question, but my heart swells when she responds.

"I love you, Dyl."

Chapter Twenty-One

A few months later

We've been through so much in the past few months. Marie was found guilty of assault, battery, sexual assault, and stalking. She admitted of her own free will she was the one who had been following Dylan since he started the show. She's the one who had been sending pictures to the Gossip Girl account.

There's been a calmness since she was sentenced to thirty years in prison with no chance of early release. Not only between Dylan and I, everyone who has ever been a part of the show, the original and current company have all been supportive. Hell, the original male lead—which let me say that was a wild experience to meet him when I've listened to his voice every day just as I had with Marie for over a year now. The original lead admitted that she had tried to do something similar to him which is why he left as soon as he could.

Men never talk about being assaulted because fewer people believe them than they believe women when they come out about sexual assault. That's why she was able to get away with it before, who knows just how many times it's happened in the past. Now, at least she won't be able to get her hands on anyone else.

I let out a nervous breath, standing in front of a full length mirror I lift my gaze and stare with my mouth a gape. My gown is off the shoulder with a sweetheart neckline, a navy blue beaded bodice that transforms into an icy blue ombre, and a mermaid skirt. It shows off my curves in the most flattering way.

"Habanero, are you ready? The car will be here in a minute." Dylan calls from the living room.

He steps in the doorway, pausing briefly when he catches sight of me. I spin to face him, my cheeks flush under his scrutinizing gaze. Dylan's eyes roam up and down my body without speaking.

"What do you think?" I ask, while I nervously brush my hands down the skirt. "Is it too much?"

He shakes his head, a mischievous grin tugs at his lips when he saunters toward me.

"I think we should skip the award show and stay home."

Laughter bubbles up from my chest. I hold my hands up in front of me.

"Stay where you are. This is a huge night for you, we're not staying home." I take a step forward and press my pink painted lips against his leaving a slight stain. "You can peel the dress off of me later."

Dylan's arms snake around my waist, his hands cup my ass as he buries his face in my neck.

"Let's go get this night over with so I can have you to myself sooner." He groans and presses a deliberate kiss against the sensitive skin where my shoulder and neck meet making my body tremble with delight.

I glance around in awe, there are celebrities of all calibers surrounding us. We're at the Tony's. It's the first time Dylan has ever been nominated. Although Her Final Shot has been nominated in nearly every category they can be. I am filled with pride knowing how much we've both been through. Separately and as a couple during the past few months that I've been living here. I'm proud of how far he's come, how much work he's put into himself, and into us when most guys would have shut down or pushed me away. At least, that's how it's been in my experience.

A roar of applause drags me from my thoughts and I glance up to see Venus Van Trager in a stunning pink sequin number standing on stage. Dylan's hand has been wrapped around mine since we've been sitting here but now, he's squeezing harder. I giggle silently to myself and wrap my free hand around both of ours.

"You've got this, my love." I whisper.

His lips pull into a tight smile and he nods acknowledging me.

"Alright y'all, settle down. We don't have all night." Venus teases the crowd when the applause continues for longer than they're comfortable with. "Tonight, we are here celebrating the best of the best on stage. We all share a unique love for this thing called show, as they say and the following group of talented performers are no different. Without further ado, the nominees for best male performance in a musical are…"

My ability to comprehend the world around me vanishes when the drumroll begins. A dramatic meaningful pause blankets the room while we wait with bated breath for the winner to be announced.

"The award goes to…Dylan Bryant for his role as Stuart Macher in Her Final Shot!"

A thunderous applause echoes throughout the theatre. I glance over to Dylan whose face has drained of color.

"Holy shit!" I squeak.

Dylan turns to me, his hands cup my cheeks as he pulls me in, pecking several quick kisses against my lips.

"I'm so proud of you!"

His grin is infectious as he stands. He steps into the aisle and strides with purpose toward the stage.

My palms sting from how hard I'm clapping, cheering for my man. Tears prick at the corners of my eyes. I glance up when a woman next to me in a black gown pats my leg and hands me a tissue. She's got a knowing smile on her face.

"Thank you." I accept the offering without looking up, grateful for the kind gesture.

"You're welcome, Mads." She winks at me.

My gaze drifts back to her after I dry my eyes. Confused, since we've never spoken before, let alone have I introduced myself. She smirks and leans in whispering low enough that only I can hear.

"xoxo, Broadway."

I suck in a lung full of air and my eyes go wide, but she nods toward the stage where my man stands. Dylan's bright blue eyes lock on mine as soon as he steps up to the mic. He holds the spinning medallion award in his arm, cradling it like it's the most precious thing he owns. After clearing his throat, he begins his acceptance speech.

"This is -" Dylan shakes his head, an air of amusement about him, "-wow. Thank you to Annie, my friend and the best Monica we could have ever hoped for. The entire company, creative team, orchestra and crew. The level of my performance wouldn't be anywhere near what I've been able to achieve without this incredible group of people." He shakes his head while his lips pull into a grateful smile. "Without each and every one of you by my side over these past eight months."

He swallows thickly and smirks at me before continuing.

"Most importantly, my gorgeous Habanero. Mads, my incredible girl-friend and love of my life. I am thankful that everyday I get to cherish you and see you blossom into even more of a badass than you were the day you stepped into my life."

Chapter Twenty-Two

Ten nominations.

Eight wins.

An unforgettable night with a group of people who have ingrained themselves so thoroughly into my life. That fact and the smile on Mads face as she sways to the beat of the music through the sound system are the only reasons I haven't snuck away from this after-party yet. She hasn't left the dance floor once since we got here; the way her body moves is hypnotizing.

A strong hand lands on my shoulder, I glance up to see the show's director, Brayden Fontane.

"You look like you're about to ravage her right here." He chuckles darkly, "Get out of here so I don't lose my second leading actor to jail time."

I choke out a laugh.

"There is something so wrong with you, Brayden."

He shrugs and nods toward Mads.

"Maybe, but sometimes laughter is the best way to get over something so traumatic. Now get the hell out of here and go be with your girl."

Our fingers are tangled together as I spin Mads around in the open space of our bedroom. She leans against me, her back against my front as we sway to the chorus of the outside world and our own breaths. I press my mouth against the sensitive skin where her neck and shoulder meet. A sweet, needy sound escapes when my lips trail soft kisses along the expanse of her exposed flesh. My hands glide along her sides until I find her dress's zipper. I smirk as my fingers linger on the metal tab. She becomes impatient, grinding her curvaceous ass against my already rock-hard cock. I suppress a chuckle and drag the tab down to uncover her smooth skin.

"You are absolutely perfect, Habanero." I whisper as soon as the dress lands on the floor, revealing she's been bare this entire time underneath.

"You are being infuriatingly sluggish tonight." She groans and turns in my arms to face me. Her full breasts and soft stomach press firmly against my front, allowing the heat from her body to soak into mine.

A smile dances on my lips when I see the annoyed expression. I lower my hands to grip her full thighs, and I lift her into my arms. She squeals in surprise as I carry her across the room, which turns into an infectious giggle.

The way her body reacts when I toss her onto the bed fills me with pride. She enjoys it more than she's ever admitted out loud. But I pay attention to every little detail when it involves Mads. She lifts herself onto her elbows, a soft smile filled with anticipation spreading across her lips.

I take a step closer to where she lies on the bed. Mads allows her legs to drop open, giving me a full view of her glistening cunt. I drag my hand down my face, pausing on my chin to scratch the scruff.

"Fuck," I groan, dragging out the word.

Her brow arches as her gorgeous chocolate eyes drift down my body. Silently asking why I'm still clothed. I chuckle, taking my time to slowly strip. She groans and drops back onto the bed.

"I hate you." She grumbles under her breath, draping her arm over her face.

"No, you don't." I kick off my shoes and hook my fingers into my slacks before pushing them down where they pool around my ankles.

"If you're not buried inside me in the next five seconds, I absolutely do hate you."

"So needy tonight, Habanero." I tease.

She mumbles something under her breath that I don't quite catch, but before she can complain further, I climb onto the bed between her open thighs. A gasp passes between her lips when she feels my hands on her thick, creamy thighs. She drops her arm and glances up at me, a smile tugging at the corner of her lips.

My hard length rests on her belly when I lean in, pressing a long kiss against her lips. I drag my fingers lightly up her side; she shivers from my touch. She moans greedily into my mouth when my hand cups her perfectly perky tit.

I nudge the head of my cock against her entrance, which pulls a whimper from my girl. My chest rumbles with sounds of my own pleasure as

I slowly fill her inch by inch. Mads' arms snake under my arms and wrap around my shoulders. She digs her nails into my back, and drags them down to my ass. She holds on tight, urging me to go harder.

My cock pulses inside her as she bucks her hips, matching me with every thrust. Pleasure builds at the base of my spine with every movement. Her legs wrap tighter around my waist, her feet digging into my ass.

"Please," her voice is soft when she begs, only gaining volume when she continues. "Fuck me like you mean it."

I glare at her, which brings a knowing smile to her face.

"I'll give you, *like I mean it.*" My tone comes across flat.

She whines needily when I slowly pull all the way out of her and turn her onto her stomach. She pulls her knees toward her, treating me to my favorite view, her ass raised in the air waiting and ready for whatever I want to do to her. I bring my right hand down, slapping her smooth skin before I part her cheeks. She sucks in a breath as I lean forward, my tongue swirling around the tight ring of muscle.

"Fuck me!" She whimpers. "Stop teasing me!"

I chuckle and reposition myself behind her. Mads reaches for my right hand; our fingers intertwine when she glances over her shoulder at me. The expression etched across her features is pure lust and desire.

My lips twitch into a smug grin as I thrust inside her to the hilt. She moans loudly at the sudden intrusion. Instead of giving her time to adjust, I find a rhythm, pulling my hips back just far enough before I rut back inside her.

The sounds she makes send a thrill of pleasure to my balls. Her walls begin to squeeze my dick, a sign that she's nearly ready to come. However, it's not until I hear the click and intense vibration from her wand that I lose a sense of control.

When the fuck did she even grab that?

"Dylan!" she shouts just as she finds her release, her pussy becomes so tight the corners of my vision go dark.

I thrust once, twice, three more times. Her cunt is still choking my cock when I find my own release. We both collapse onto the mattress. Mads shoulders shake with silent laughter.

"Ok, I don't hate you anymore."

Chapter Twenty-Three

A rush of air caresses my bare arms when Enid passes by me in a blur while she hurries to finish putting the final touches on the decor for tonight. We've been working together since I moved here to get more author-centric events here at The Shredded Bodice. Today is the first time that I'm recording my podcast live with an author and an audience of readers for in-person questions and conversation, and to say I am ecstatic is an understatement.

I blow out a shaky breath. Anxiety has been tormenting me all day. No one has called me out on it yet, thankfully. You'd think with as many episodes as I've recorded I wouldn't get nervous anymore. That may be true under normal circumstances however this is far from the norm.

If anyone has been with me physically while recording it's been Elle or Fallon so this - this is new.

I check my laptop and mics for what feels like the tenth time when there's a soft knock at the door. My gaze drifts up just in time to see the familiar face of someone I've only ever chatted with online or via text, and a wide grin spreads across my face. A similar excitement brightens her jade-green eyes as soon as she catches sight of me. B. Kitt, an author I've been crushing on — because of her writing, though she is gorgeous, but don't make it weird — agreed to come all the way out to Brooklyn from the Midwest for this episode. She's been a guest multiple times, and I've given her an open invite to come back for any new releases she has. Are author crushes a thing? I think they're a thing.

"Ahh! It's so good to meet you in person!" B rushes toward me, her arms spread wide, and she pulls me into a warm embrace.

I chuckle, returning the hug, and step back. Excitement is now vibrating through me that she's here and I'm suddenly no longer anxious.

"It's been a long time coming! Tonight is going to be amazing. Are you ready?"

She nods enthusiastically, and I guide her to one of the oversized pink armchairs.

As soon as Enid gives the all-clear for our ticketed guests, a group of ten people who won tickets after submitting how B's books have changed their lives. Not necessarily sexually, but she did consent to people getting dirty if her stories have helped their sex lives.

If you've been introduced to Daddy Aiden, you'd understand just how much her writing could positively affect your extracurricular activities.

We wait until everyone has taken their seats before we begin. We may not have met in person before, but I can see the nerves beginning to get to her. I squeeze her hand and smile to let her know she's not alone.

"Hey everyone! Thank you so much for coming out tonight to what we hope is just the first of a bi-monthly series of live recordings for "O"—The Positive Side of Smut podcast here at The Shredded Bodice!" I greet our guests. "Now, I know I'm pretty awesome, but let's talk about the real reason we're all excited to be here tonight."

I gesture toward B who waves excitedly to everyone.

"B. Kitt, the author of one of my favorite books and the best spicy novella you'll ever get your hands on."

There may only be ten people in attendance tonight, but you'd never be able to tell based on how loud the cheering is.

From the time I press record to the time we're done, we've spent several hours talking about everything from books, writing, life, sex, and everything in between on top of taking reader questions. I have so much content it will be enough for a two-part special.

Each person who has come in to be part of this special milestone for my show is surprised with a limited print special leather-bound foil cover edition omnibus of B's Aurora Duet.

One woman who has been most engaged tonight is so shocked that she faints.

Well, shit.

Thankfully, she comes to quickly and is perfectly fine, only a little embarrassed.

"I guess we went a little too hard." I say to B and shrug, which makes us both laugh.

A throat clears from behind us and I glance toward the newcomer to find a gorgeous, tall, muscular hunk of a man with a glint of mischief in his light blue eyes. He smirks at me as soon as he sees my attention is on him.

"Damn, Habanero." His gaze trails down my body to a blue tank top that hugs my curves and a pair of dark cut-off shorts showing off my thighs. "How am I supposed to take you to meet Ka'Mani for dinner if you look like that? Gorgeous, you look like you could be dinner."

I shake my head, giggling at his remarks.

"Dylan, this is B. Kitt. B, my boyfriend, Dylan." I introduce the two of them.

"God, damn, woman. You won the lottery of men. Good for you." She fans herself dramatically. "No, really, can I put you in a book?"

She directs the question toward Dylan whose cheeks turn bright red at her request. My eyes light up as I take the few steps to where he stands. Once I get in front of him, I place my hands on his chest and stare up at him with my own sinful smile.

"Yes! We need you in the book world, what do you say, Daddy..." I pause to see how the term affects him - his gaze darkens as he looks down at me. A glint of mischief that I can't wait to unpack later, "Dylan."

Chapter Twenty-Four

One Year Later

Over the past three months, a plan has been forming in my mind. I've shared the idea with only one person, and he's been giving me shit for just as long. Mr. Phillips is choking back laughter while I pace nervously in front of his carriage. The horse, Mr. Ed, is side eyeing me with a judgmental stare.

"Well, hello there, handsome." The voice of my favorite person sounds from behind me, her mere presence causing a flutter in my stomach.

I still, and turn to see Mads. She's stunning as always. My heart beats faster when I see what she's wearing; a short black skirt barely covering her ass, though today she's wearing fishnet stockings and a burnt orange sweater. The very same outfit from our first date.

"Trying to make me jealous again, Habanero?" I snort and take a few steps to wrap my arms around her. "You look amazing."

Mads' lips turn up into a warm smile at my compliment.

"But you're missing something." I wink before stepping over to the carriage and to pull something I stashed when Mr. Phillips and I first arrived.

Her dark eyes shine with emotion when I wrap the same jacket I had given her during our first date.

"Happy anniversary, my love." I lean down and press my lips to hers.

"Aww, thanks, kid." Mr. Phillips' usually grumpy voice sounds soft and sentimental.

I shake my head while I try to fight back a smirk. I offer my arm to Mads, guiding her to the carriage. She stops to say "hello" but mostly it's to pet the horse before she allows me to help her up.

"Hi, sweetheart, it's good to see you again." His warm greeting toward her is more in line with what I'd expect from the older man.

Once she's seated, I climb up and join her. I pull her tight into my embrace; our legs brush against one another, my warmth enveloping her. Mads nuzzles into me, her head resting in the crook of my neck.

With a quick click of the tongue from Mr. Phillips, we're off.

My gaze drifts over the park's landscape. What feels like endless rolling hills, boulders, trails and over a hundred statues. When Mads' first moved here, she would take the train from our place in Brooklyn to Manhattan just to spend a day in the park. I know she misses being surrounded by nature. I've joined her on more than one occasion. Especially after everything that happened with Marie. Knowing she was out on her own made me more anxious than I care to admit. However, it was during one of those trips that she confessed her favorite place in the park is the Alice in Wonderland statue.

There's a nostalgia to it that brings her peace. Her mom would put her to bed when she was little while they listened to the story on vinyl.

Our conversation flows as easily as it always does. However, this morning, my mind is running rampant with anticipation. When the carriage comes to a stop by the conservatory water, I help her step down while Mr. Phillips waits.

"You know," I begin when we walk toward the steps that lead to the Wonderland statue. "The first time I saw you, you were sitting in the front row. I told Cassie that I needed to meet you."

My palms are sweating. I wipe my hands down my pants before I place my hand on the small of her back, guiding her forward.

"I remember." Her voice is so soft.

"Well, it turns out, I need so much more than that." I cup her hands in mine. Her stunning dark stare makes my heart race. "It turns out I need the rest of my life with you."

Her dark eyes go wide when I drop to a knee and display a small book with a floral foil design. I flip the top open to reveal a nature-inspired black gold ring. The design has small twigs and leaves curving around a two-carat diamond.

"Maddox Joy Davis, will you -?"

"Are you serious?" She chokes; tears stream down her cheeks.

"Yes, Habanero." I nod; my lips pull into a smile.

Mads squeals, her arms fling around my neck.

"Yes, Dylan, yes!" she cries into my neck. "Nothing would make me happier."

I wrap my arms around her as she cries.

"Can I put this ring on your finger now?" I whisper the question in her ear. "I've had this thing burning a hole in my pocket for months, and I've been going crazy for it to be on you."

She giggles and pulls away. A look of wonder on her face as I slide it into place.

"How did you manage to keep this from me?" Mads chokes on a sob.

I glance over to Mr. Phillips, who has my phone pointed to us. He's been dutifully recording the entire event from his carriage.

"I had a little help." A chuckle escapes my lips.

Mads' lips pull up into a wide grin.

"Well, I guess he did help you get the first date. He may as well be involved in securing the rest of your life."

Laughter erupts from both of us as we return to the carriage.

"Much smoother this time, kid." Mr. Phillips jabs when he hands me my phone when we approach.

I roll my eyes, knowing he will never let me live down how our first date went. My gaze drags over Mads when we're back in the carriage. Her eyes stay trained on the ring, admiringly. I lean in and press my lips to her ear.

"I can't wait to see you in just that ring."

A shiver runs through her body. She tries to glare at me from under her lashes, but she's unable to hide the needy smile that I've grown to know so well. I grin to myself knowing that this is just the beginning of our lives together.

Forever can't come soon enough.

Epilogue

Six years later

Smoke clouds linger as I rush into the kitchen. I hurry to the sink for a towel to wave the hazy air away. Cursing under my breath, I open the oven to see a burnt frozen pizza.

"Habanero, my love? I know you like things spicy but I thought we had an unspoken agreement not to burn the house down." Dylan calls from the hall.

"You're the one that knocked me up again." I glare in the direction of his voice. "You know what pregnancy brain does to me!"

My entire nervous system goes through an automatic reboot when I catch a glimpse of him bare chested carrying our two-year-old, Bodie.

Our little boy is curled up against his daddy, content and by the looks of it, starting to doze. We've been married going on five years, and I still have the desire to mount him every time I see him.

Our engagement only lasted six months before Dylan and I decided we didn't want to do an elaborate wedding. He may have some celebrity status and to some extent so do I but neither of us needed a grand event. When he made the suggestion of doing it at the theatre on a day they had off, it felt like kismet.

My friends from home flew out and made it an incredible experience. With Dylan's connections he was able to get a hold of someone to help me find a dress and have it altered in only a week.

We had talked about waiting a few years before trying for kids, but Dylan barely lasted until our first wedding anniversary before he begged me to make him a dad.

Damn, did we have fun trying, but the universe had other plans for us and didn't grant that wish until three years in, which is when we moved back home — to Hollow Heights.

Since we've been here, Dylan's creative mind has been going a million miles a minute. He needed an outlet, and after reading so many of my books, so he knew what I would go on about, he decided to try his hand at writing. The fact that he is multifaceted in the creative aspects of his life is astounding.

After only publishing for a year and a half, he has ten titles out with most having been on the best seller list. His popularity has only grown since he decided to co-host the podcast with me. Giving a unique insight on the open-minded male brain.

Fuck, he is sexy when he talks smut and is one of the few men who isn't condescending or condemning when the topic arises.

"Stop looking at me like that, gorgeous." Dylan warns when he rejoins me after putting Bodie down for a nap, "Elle is going to be here soon to take over so we can record. You've been talking about our episode with Nikki for weeks."

"Please, Daddy?" I pout. "You can use my mouth so one of us can get relief."

His eyes darken, the familiar excitement any time I call him that in a playful way.

"Habanero, you know damn well you would have to redo your hair and makeup, and we would be late."

I step toward him, and my gaze rakes up his chiseled form. He looks just as good as the day we first met. I drag my nails down his chest and raise onto my tip toes to press my lips to his in a quick kiss.

"Maybe, but it would be worth it."

His head lulls back between his shoulders when my fingers reach his waist band, a throaty growl rumbles free.

A soft knock on the door is the only warning we have before Elle and her husband walk in like they own the place. Granted we all just walk into one another's. All of us having kids now has made it so we're less likely to walk in on anyone in a compromising position.

"You have three seconds to be decent, we're coming in!" Elle calls with her hand clasped over her eyes.

I let out a boisterous laugh when she stumbles over her own feet as their daughter rushes past her.

"Shit! Damnit!" Her husband narrowly misses her, but she somehow gracefully lands on the couch.

"Why are y'all still here? Go do your thing. We got this." She shoos us with her hand. "He's napping for at least two hours, give him a snack

when he wakes up, don't burn the house down - it's not our first rodeo."
She snorts.

After I go back into Bodie's room to check on him and a quick farewell
to our friends, we step into the back yard and walk the few paces to our
studio. We had it built when we bought the house.

It reminds me of what a sheshack meeting a tiny house would be like.
We made sure the structure had soundproofing before allowing the build
to begin. The two long walls are painted a deep charcoal while the other
two are a deep pink. There is everything you could want here, a kitchenette, bathroom, not only is it where we record, Dylan has transformed
it into a reading nook and a place to create content.

He is already getting the computer up when I stop daydreaming about
how perfect our life has been. Piercing blue eyes land on me as I step
around, my hand is resting on my protruding belly. His expression softens when I step into his space and he wraps an arm around my waist
while we wait for everything to load.

It only takes five minutes until we're ready to go.

My heart beats quickly with excitement when I see Nikki Grant, an
author I've been following for years pop onto our screen. We spend a few
minutes chatting before we begin recording. Dylan winks at me when
it's time for me to begin.

"Hey there Bestie's! It's Mads' on mic with another episode of
"O"–The Positive Side of Smut."

Scan for all additional titles

About the Author

I'm an introvert. Well, until you get to know me. Then I won't shut up. I'm married to my favorite PITA; he's the doctor to my Clara. (IYKYK). We have a little boy who is growing way too fast and is already way too smart for my own sanity. I've had an unhealthy obsession with

Gilmore Girls and *Buffy the Vampire Slayer* for years. You'll see the references throughout my writing. I've loved reading for as long as I can remember, but physical books with traditional novel paper give me the ick! So, you'll find me reading on my Kindle or listening to audiobooks on the regular.

Be sure to stalk me on all of my socials here

Acknowledgements

My family, your support during this journey has been incredible.

To my Stupid Face Moron, ditto.

My alpha team, you are the MVP, and I can't imagine this journey without you.

Sara - My boo. I'll forever be thankful that you slid into my DM's. You are phenomenal, and I love you!

Brittany – From 0-2mil and for the rest of the ride. You are one of my favorite humans and I'm so thankful to know you.... & for Abelina.

Tana – I'll never be able to thank you enough for the way you've curbed the chaos that is my mind.

K.D. - My ride or die, I love you, and I'm so freaking proud of you!

My Street Team – Bestie Boo's:

Laura P., Brittany T., Jennifer L., Nicole H., Jessi H., Tabs S., Jasmine G., Jeanette R., Erin V., Becci T., Lindsey M., Erin S., Brandy S., Christina, Clarissa D., Faiza J., Summer M.

Without y'all I don't know where I'd be. You are the best group of people a girl could ask for. <3

To the FBI Agent who tracks my search history, you're welcome for the break this time around.

Lastly, but most definitely not least, to every single one of you who has reached this page. There will never be enough words for me to express my love for you adequately. Thank you for reading my books. I can't wait to share additional stories with you!